AND THE WHALE IS OURS

AND
THE WHALE
IS OURS

CREATIVE WRITING
OF AMERICAN WHALEMEN

BY PAMELA A. MILLER

DAVID R. GODINE · PUBLISHER
BOSTON · MASSACHUSETTS

THE KENDALL WHALING MUSEUM
SHARON · MASSACHUSETTS

PUBLISHED BY
DAVID R. GODINE, PUBLISHER, INC.
306 DARTMOUTH STREET
BOSTON, MASSACHUSETTS 02116

Special thanks to the following institutions for granting permission to quote from their journals and other works:
Collection of the International Marine Archives, Nantucket, Massachusetts; Essex Institute, Salem, Massachusetts; Houghton Library, Harvard University, Cambridge, Massachusetts; The Kendall Whaling Museum, Sharon, Massachusetts; Manuscript Collection, Mystic Seaport, Inc., Mystic, Connecticut; The Mariner's Museum, Newport News, Virginia; New Bedford Free Public Library, New Bedford, Massachusetts; Nicholson Whaling Collection, Providence Public Library, Providence, Rhode Island; Old Dartmouth Historical Society and Whaling Museum, New Bedford, Massachusetts; The Peabody Museum of Salem, Salem, Massachusetts; Peter Foulger Museum, Nantucket Historical Association, Nantucket, Massachusetts.

All of the illustrations in this book are reproduced with permission from The Kendall Whaling Museum, Sharon, Massachusetts.

ISBN: 0-87923-252-8
LCC NO: 78-58449

Manufactured in the United States of America

TABLE OF CONTENTS

ACKNOWLEDGMENTS

In putting this book together, I have relied on the knowledge, skill, and goodwill of many people. Special thanks must go to the Kendall Whaling Museum, whose magnificent manuscript collection initially inspired my search, and whose interest in this topic made my book possible. The index to the collection, compiled by Mrs. Dorothy Brewington (now of Mystic Seaport, Mystic, Connecticut), first made me aware of the wealth of available material. The museum's director, Dr. Kenneth R. Martin, has been constantly helpful with his enthusiasm, knowledge of whaling, and attention to detail.

I especially appreciate the courtesy and cooperation of those who facilitated my search: Mrs. Virginia Adams, Special Collections, Providence Public Library, Providence, Rhode Island; Mr. Bruce Barnes, Curator, Melville Whaling Room, New Bedford Free Public Library, New Bedford, Massachusetts; Mr. Robert H. Ellis, Jr., Registrar, Ms. Rebecca L. Jackson, Research Associate, The Kendall Whaling Museum, Sharon, Massachusetts; Mr. Douglass C. Fonda, Jr., International Marine Archives, Nantucket, Massachusetts; Mr. Richard C. Kugler, Director, Old Dartmouth Historical Society and Whaling Museum, New Bedford, Massachusetts; Mr. Douglas L. Stein, Manuscript Librarian, and Mrs. Virginia Coope, Mystic Seaport, Mystic, Connecticut; and Mr. Edouard A. Stackpole, Director, The Peter Foulger Museum, Nantucket, Massachusetts.

Professor Harrison T. Meserole, of the Pennsylvania State University, has encouraged me in this project from its beginnings. I have profited from his comprehensive knowledge and enjoyed his wit. Two other colleagues, Professors Deborah S. Austin and Shirley Marchalonis, also read the manuscript and made helpful comments.

One person in particular stands out: Doris Skawden Croskey. To say that she typed the manuscript does not begin to describe her contribution. Her painstaking care, especially in reproducing the whalemen's writing exactly, was the work of a scholar and a friend.

INTRODUCTION

PAMELA MILLER is a literature specialist of exceptional discernment. Respectful of American literary jewels, she nonetheless possesses a regard for the semiprecious: popular writing of the nineteenth century. Ms. Miller is also authoritative on Yankee whaling history. This is fortuitous, for who else would hunt for diamonds – or rhinestones – in a woodpile of more than 3,500 whaling manuscripts? The result of her work is a readable volume of wide appeal and substantial scholarship.

And the Whale Is Ours reflects a recent trend which turns from preoccupation with classics to consideration of popular works which influenced more of American society than did rarified masterpieces. In this anthology, almost all of which is previously unpublished, Ms. Miller clearly demonstrates the connection between popular reading and amateur inspiration.

The book humanizes that vague entity, the Yankee whaleman, without resorting to traditional romanticism. In doing so, it illuminates some peculiar aspects of the nineteenth century whale fishery, historically one of America's most important but most misunderstood industries.

And the Whale Is Ours is a rare item: a stylish book of real interest to scholars and casual readers. The Kendall Whaling Museum is proud to make this volume the first of its new series.

Kenneth R. Martin
Director
The Kendall Whaling Museum

AND THE WHALE IS OURS

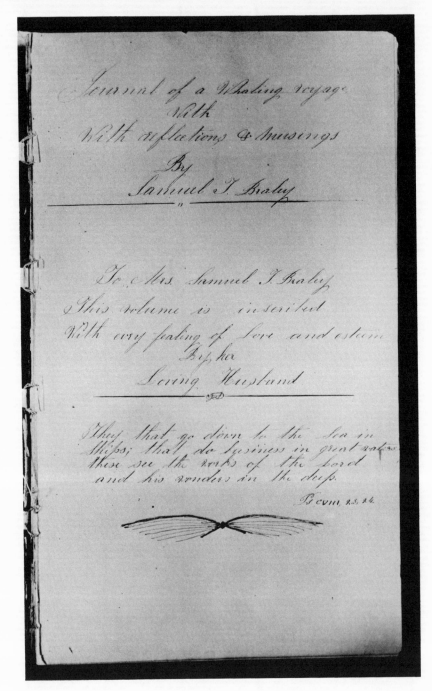

Something of Captain Samuel Braley's character and inspiration to write may be seen in the title page of this journal, kept on board the *Arab*, 1850–1852.

PREFACE

Poem by B F Rogers

it was the 14th day of April
i remember well the day
as our gallang little schoonr
lay at anchor in the bay
our hearts were light and bouyant
as we striped ourselves for toil
it is heave up the anchor boys
and of we go for oil[1]

BENJAMIN F. ROGERS of Chicago sailed in 1863 on his first whaling voyage aboard the schooner *V. H. Hill*. Rogers's journal, now at The Kendall Whaling Museum of Sharon, Massachusetts, is one of nearly 3,500 whaling logbooks and journals* that exist today in major American public collections. These records have become increasingly valuable over the years, primarily for their human interest, historical data, and colorful illustrations.

Like Rogers, a number of the men who kept these records spent a great deal of time experimenting with creative writing. Their work has until now been virtually ignored. This anthology includes selections from 42 writers, the most typical and most important examples of original creative writing from journals that survive in public collections.

These writers lived in the most productive era of American whaling; their writings particularly represent the 1840's and 1850's. Most were officers, or officers-to-be. All were apparently white, native-born Americans.

* *Although 'logbook' is now strictly defined as the official record of a ship's business and travels kept by the first officer, whalemen used the terms 'logbook' and 'journal' synonymously to refer to their shipboard diaries.[2] To avoid confusion, both logbooks and journals will hereafter be referred to as 'journals.'*

Their education and abilities differed enormously: some of the selections are skillful and polished, others rough, misspelled, and crude.

Like writers on shore, they often take as their subjects home, love, and death. But even more frequently, the substance of their daily lives becomes their theme. Despite the conditions of mental and physical hardship widespread throughout the industry, few entries speak of unhappiness or self-pity. Most of their work is straightforward, uncritical, even light-hearted prose and verse describing life on board ship and the processes of whaling.

As much as possible, the selections are drawn from original material written on board ship by whalemen who did not intend to publish immediately, if at all, rather than those who wrote highly descriptive narratives of dramatic whale chases and foreign ports for hometown newspapers. These are the obscure journal keepers who consciously attempted literary expression for their own pleasure, or that of their friends and families.

Determining the originality of the one drama, the essays, the several novellas, and the substantial amount of poetry I selected from these journals was at times a complicated problem. Some work was obviously topical and personal. But many whalemen copied poetry into their journals, and others practiced their handwriting by copying from well-known writers and from newspapers. Some transcribed songs they heard during gams (visits between whaleships at sea) or in their own forecastles. Such notations as 'written on board the *Globe*, July 14, 1820, by a whaleman' are frequently untrustworthy as guarantees of authentically original work. Written indeed it may have been, at the time and the place described, but as a handwriting exercise.

Even if a work was not clearly a copy of a well-known poem or a popular parlor song or ballad, it was still sometimes difficult to determine its authenticity. The mass of facile verse and fiction published during whaling's heyday, in yearbooks, albums, storypapers, and newspapers, was far too great to make positive identification certain. Besides material which had obviously been copied, I discarded any work appearing more than once in journals by different men or on different voyages.

This process eliminated many items from consideration. The individual journals themselves provided further clues. Did the general style and handwriting of the daily entries match those of the creative work? Often they did not. And often it is clear that the pages at the back are the work of other hands. But diction and handwriting were not positive means of identification, either. The play, essays, fiction, and poetry are more consciously 'literary' than their authors' daily entries in all but a few cases.

In addition, journals were often written under varying conditions which created physical difficulties. Richard M. Hixson, an inland New Englander on his first whaling voyage, wrote a preface at the end of his journal describing these problems. He begins mildly enough, but grows angry as he defends his work from the criticism of 'grumbletonians.'

Preface.

I think it better to have a preface at the end of this journal than to have none at all, for the following reason viz to let those who may read this book after I am forgotten know, I can if I should try, write a better composition can spell a little better, and finely I can write a better hand – This question will naturally arise, Why did you not do all this while keeping your journal? I answer in the first place I thought I would merely keep a memorandum of some of the most important events that would take place in the course of the voiage on which I was about commencing. In the next place I was not capable of keeping so correct a journal on board a ship as I should have been in a convenient place on shore. It was a long time before I became acquainted with the motion of the ship so that I could write at all – A considerable of this part of the journal was wrote in gleles of winds; other parts when I was in a hurry, and but a little at my leisure – I took no pains to arraign what I was about to write, but put down whatever came first in mind that had transpired – I do not pretend that I can write correctly, I acknowledge that I am a blunderhead, all I wish to say is, that I can do a little better than I have don in this book – And now gentle reader you may believe what I have here advanced or disbelieve it. I do not care a fig, I kept the journal for my own amusement and am perfectly satisfied – So farewell grumbletonian you get no satisfaction from, Maria at sea   Richard M. Hixson Dec 30th 1834[3]]

Hixson's prose is fairly representative of most selections in this anthology. Because of the difficulties he describes, or because of lack of education, the punctuation, grammar, and spelling are often irregular.

Some writers' punctuation may simply mark places where a pen rested; some writers regularly substituted one letter for another. In a few cases, then, my final decision on an item's originality was based on matching individual quirks of diction or spelling with those in daily journal entries. If they and the handwriting were at least roughly similar, I did not quibble further. In all cases, the selections are reproduced here exactly as they appeared in the journals. Only in the most puzzling cases have I noted irregularities.

Beyond the question of originality lies that of quality. I attempted above all to select those works which capture something of the vigor and the routine, the camaraderie and the loneliness of life on board a Yankee whaling ship.

CHAPTER ONE

AGAIN I AM ON THE DEEP

WHALING in North America began with the American Indians, who ventured from shore in canoes to hunt whales near the coastlines. Such whaling was sporadic; not until the influx of European settlers did whaling become a systematic business endeavor. By the eighteenth century, small coastal communities in southern New England began sending out specially equipped vessels on extended voyages to capture the whales that had learned to avoid coastal waters. Eventually, there were whaleships hailing from such unlikely ports as Poughkeepsie, New York; Wilmington, Delaware; and Newark, New Jersey. But the vast majority of whalers sailed from ports in New England where fishing could easily compete with farming.

The industry reached its peak in the decades between 1820 and the American Civil War. From a small, localized industry, in which individual towns often banded together to send out ships manned by local youths, whaling became mechanized and impersonal – one of America's major industries.[1] The kind of whaling described in Melville's *Moby Dick*, carried out by a multinational crew on board a floating whale-oil factory, was typical of the industry only during its mid-nineteenth-century boom.

Then came the Civil War. Confederate vessels chased and destroyed many Yankee whaleships, and the North itself deliberately sunk the forty Yankee whalers of the Great Stone Fleet to blockade the harbors of Charleston and Savannah. After the War, other ship losses came from extending whaling to Arctic grounds: at least 45 vessels were lost in the ice during the 1870's. The final blow to the industry came with the discovery of petroleum and natural gas. By the 1880's, cheap substitutes for spermaceti candles and whale-oil lubricants swamped the market. And as prices for whale products declined, American industry on shore expanded.

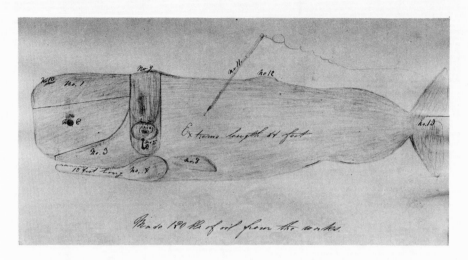

The most dangerous quarry: a colossal bull sperm whale. From Joseph Hersey's journal.

Cotton mills and heavy industry became the new sources of wealth, attracting the young and ambitious.[2]

Whaling on a minor scale lingered on into the 1920's. But in 1925, the schooner *John R. Manta* tied up at New Bedford, and the last Yankee whaling voyage was over. Only one wooden whaleship still exists, the restored *Charles W. Morgan*, which is on permanent display at Mystic Seaport.

Shore whaling and the early short voyages seldom produced any written records. As voyages stretched into years, however, legal records became necessary and journal keeping became an important pastime. The earliest known manuscript journals cover voyages made in 1751.[3] As the number of voyages increased, so did the number of journals. Of the 13,927 known American whaling voyages, perhaps as many as one-third are covered by journals surviving in public and private ownership.[4]

The survival of whaling journals was chancy. Logbooks, stored for reference by ships' agents, were often discarded as companies changed ownership or closed down. William Kranzler of New Bedford, an antique dealer since the 1920's, remembers seeing stacks of logbooks for sale as scrap paper for as little as a nickel a pound.[5] Private journals naturally remained the property of their writers. Although many of these were treasured by descendants of whalemen, and some were presented to local historical societies, many more were discarded or lost.

Most of the American whaling journals that have survived are stored in public collections on the East Coast. Although some museums have begun

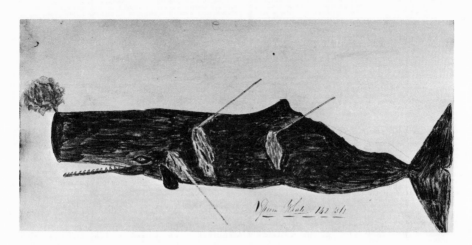

A more ferocious approach to a similar subject. From George Gould's
Columbia journal. The bull's size, expressed in barrels of oil, is probably
wishful thinking.

the long, expensive process of restoring the documents, few journals are in
good condition. Many journalists took home their manuscripts to use as
scrapbooks or scrap paper. Wives pasted in recipes. Children scribbled
over daily entries as well as the blank pages left at the end. Even when
collected in museums, the journals were not always safe. One former
curator was known to have cut out 'blank' pages to use for scratch paper.

Most whalemen journalists never expected their works to be read or
saved. Few were interested in writing other than as a daily record, and
few of the journals make interesting reading. Most lapse into an irritating
sameness, no matter what their date. Except for the occasional excitement
of taking a whale, life on board ship began and ended in routine. Daily
entries generally start with a description of the weather, briefly list the
activities of the day, and conclude with figures of latitude and longitude.
Seldom is there an attempt at any but the most dry and factual record;
perhaps only one journal out of a hundred contains even a fragment of
original creative writing, most often poetry. But some have genuine merit
as social and literary documents.

Even those whalemen who enjoyed writing and did a great deal of it
were frequently overcome with boredom and a sense of futility that daily
journal keeping seemed only to aggravate. George Mills, for example, a
mate on several whaleships in the mid-1850's, kept a journal which includes many poems and some fiction. But prolific as he was, the prospect
of recording daily life on a whaleship became impossible. His journal,
after the first forty-six pages, contains the following:

NOTICE

No, as I live. and nothing happens more than what eventfully takes place. I will not continue Log keeping no more. No how *for it is one day out and another in. Just the same. therefore Please Excuse Etc* [6]

There are no journal entries thereafter – only anecdotes, fiction, and poetry.

Almost all of the whalemen writers represented in this anthology were young. Indeed, most foremast hands were in their teens or twenties, and officers were seldom much older.[7]

Throughout the whaling era, most officers were of a similar background. The responsible posts drew young and ambitious career men, often from good families, who intended to become captains. Through the early 1800's, all hands shared this sense of dedication. Even as late as 1834, the *Ceres* of Wilmington, the first vessel of the Wilmington Whaling Company, which was owned by the shareholders of the city, set sail with a crew which included many members of the local lyceum, young men from wealthy Wilmington families.[8] Yet as the whaling industry changed during the mid-1800's, so did the whalemen. Eventually crews lost their local cohesiveness and came to be made up almost entirely of foreigners and inland Americans.[9]

Crews in the later days of Yankee whaling suffered from the exploitative, pinchpenny practices of the trade. Few men of status signed on. Some of these later whalemen were farm boys, enticed by the imagined glamour of whaling. Others were city types or freedmen unable to find other employment. Still others were former whalemen, victims of 'landsharks,' who had squandered their small wages and had no alternative but to make another voyage. A few were criminals escaping shore justice by shipping out under assumed names, and indeed, in many cases positive identification of individual crew members is guesswork.

Throughout the later days of whaling, most crewmen lived under appalling conditions. Officers fared better, with more abundant and more varied food and the privacy of cabins. Harpooners and shipboard craftsmen also enjoyed privileges. But the squalid forecastle where the crew lived was small, stuffy, and crowded. Food was monotonous, often spoiled

AGAIN I AM ON THE DEEP

or filled with weevils – and sometimes scanty. John A. States, writing on the *Nantasket* in 1845, describes that ship's forecastle and its forlorn inmates in an account that is mournful rather than embittered. But then, it was only the start of the voyage.

By the dim light of the lamp which is swinging to and fro in the gloomy forecastle may be seen a group of sleepers who worn out with fatigue and watching are now enjoying a few moments of troubled rest. Let us cast our eyes around and while they are sleeping let us read their Characters. Yonder lies four of that class of persons to whom a little money is a fortune and who are striving to amass enough to carry them to their native country. Ignorant almost as brutes they are the victims of tyranny and have not the spirit to enjoy any other than the basest of sinful pleasures still they have one redeeming quality for they are ardently attached to their home and if they are successful will eventually return to it. Beneath one of these sleeps a toil worn sailor. Left an orphan in his early years when he most needed the comforting hand of a parent he has struggled through the world to earn a scanty pittance which when received has been squandered away on objects unworthy of his regard to him life appears an alternation of sunshine and gloom. at one time revelling in the midst of sinful pleasures and at another in want of the necessaries of life He will probably struggle on never knowing what true pleasure is and perhaps finish his life in the midst of his evil courses. There is another one who with a good steady character being in want of employment and deceived as to the nature of the business has embarked and found like many others by sad experience that it is not always proper to trust to the honor of strangers With him is one in the prime of life who lives as if the present moment were his only care and whose only ambition is to be in the situation in which he is placed Beneath is one who left his home a boy and who has now grown to mans estate. He is probably dreaming of his happy home of friends and kindred. Perhaps too he dreams of her who gave him her youthful heart and his mind dwells with pleasure on the blissful fancy. Others are there some with the glowing fancies of youth and others with the riper thoughts of maturer age all sleeping and perhaps all dreaming one dreams of the preceeding days conflict when one of the monsters of the deep was captured another dreams of those pleasures which he enjoyed on his last visit to his home. Some dream of their father and mother whose gray hairs they have bowed down with sorrow by following their wayward path again another who left home with pleasing anticipations and looks forward with pleasure to the happy time when returning from sea he will be enabled to accomplish his purposes. He perhaps is thinking of pouring wealth into the lap of a thankful mother to cheer her declining days. But long months of toil must intervene and then perhaps his schemes may be frustrated. There is yet another who does not partake of even the pleasure of dreaming. He who is laid upon the bed of sickness awake and in pain. To him the hours pass slowly and drearily away No kind mothers soothing hand to smooth his pillow no sister to administer the cooling draught to stay the progress of the destroyer but alone amongst strangers he passes the dreary hours Oh then how sweet to him is the voice of friendship how pleasantly it sounds in his ear And he lifts up his heart in thankfulness to God that he has not been utterly forsaken. Time rolls along and the sleepers still continue their slumbers. When bursting upon the ear comes the hoarse notes of the summons for them to rise and renew their toil after perhaps four hours sleep. Slowly they rise their sweet dreams dissipated and themselves awake to the sad reality. Now they commence their preparations for their mornings meal out from their corners they bring their tin pots and pans and seating themselves around upon their chests each one facing his messmate await the coming of their meal Soon it comes a bucket full of boiled coffee without molasses a scanty supply of salt beef with hard wormy bread constitutes their meal and of this bad as it is they have not enough By the time their meal is finished the voice of an officer is heard and away they must hasten to the deck again to resume their slavish toil Then the foolish boy who left his home with such pleasing anticipations sighs for the comforts of his fathers house and inwardly resolves that if ever he does get home he will return like the prodigal son to the bosom of his kind parents and now when in view of his sad condition he contrasts it with former days his full heart is almost ready to burst as he thinks that at the very moment when he is in this lamentable situation his fond parents are thinking of and perhaps praying For him. But short is the time allowed for sentiment and he resumes his toilsome labor though with a sad and heavy heart. This is not altogether a dream of Fancy for but few that have been on a whaling cruise but they have often been in scenes like this.[10]

Such conditions could only increase the distance, psychological and physical, between officers and crew. Minds that were sensitive and fastidious suffered and withdrew, turning perhaps to their journals for solace. Many whalemen, officers and crew alike, clearly felt lonely on voyages which separated them for years from friends and family. And many turned to journal keeping as an emotional outlet. But aside from the basic need for expression, whalemen kept their journals for a variety of reasons. For official logbook keepers, personal commentary was a result of boredom or of unusually strong feeling. Others kept a journal, as travelers still do today, simply as a memento.

Some openly stated their reasons for journal keeping. Ambrose Bates, first mate on the New Bedford bark *Milwood*,[11] and a prolific writer in almost every literary genre, wrote to ease his loneliness:

Again I am on the deep Again I am leaveing all I hold dear in this world And many and many must be the weary day I shall pass e'er I return if ever that may be But if it be my lot to leave this form of clay upon some corral [*reef*]. *Or upon the desolate shores of a frozen zone. I shall not go unmourned for I believe there are those who would miss me many a long day. And perhaps this book may reach them and these unworthy museings of mine may cheer their remembrance of me . . . .*[12]

Another journalist, R. G. N. Swift, is more cheerful. His prefaces to two journals show his familiarity with gothic novels, Latin, and Shakespeare, as well as his sense of humor. Unlike Bates, this writer claims he writes only for himself. His preface to his first journal is buoyant:

Preface.
Scripsi in nave Conteste in annis. MDCCCLXVI,
MDCCCLXVII, et MDCCCLXVIII

This Journal is being written on board the Ship Contest and I propose to write in it an account of the occurrences, accidents, doings, exploits & & during the present whaling voyiage, especially those in which "ego ipse" am concerned

These pages are written for no one but myself, and if any one should have the temerity to read thus far; either from chance, or evil design, or natural and inherent depravity; let him pause.**** And, after this solemn warning, if he *turns over this leaf, let it be at his peril; he has chosen a course that will inevitably lead him to _____ the end of this book, if he continues reading long enough. Therefore I say, beware my vengeance.!*[13]

Swift shipped on another voyage in 1868, having advanced from the forecastle to a boatsteerer's (harpooner's) berth.[14] Despite his success, he had misgivings.

"Ay, now am I in Arden; the more fool I; when I was at home I was in a better place; but travellers must be content."
                    As you Like It

The purpose you undertake is dangerous; the time, ill sorted; the friends, not to be depended upon.
                    King Henry IV

Second Voyiage of
Sinbad the
Sailor.[15]

Style in these journals quite often followed the rank and station of crew members. Whaling captains, officers, and shipboard craftsmen such as carpenters and blacksmiths were usually better educated than forecastle hands. Moreover, they rose in the morning, worked during the day, and slept through the night. This schedule, as well as the relative privacy of their quarters, made the physical process of writing simpler. The more highly crafted poetry and complex narratives came from writers with these privileges.

The crew served watches day and night, in four-hour and two-hour periods of duty. Their creative efforts, more often oral than written, were primarily work songs or chanteys, songs about their ship, their shipmates, and their work.[16] Benjamin F. Rogers's song about the crew of the schooner *V. H. Hill* (see chapter V) is a rare example of such a song that is clearly original. Most examples in the journals are derivative, mingling lines from several songs, and changing names and other specifics to suit the writer's own circumstances.[17]

A few of the journalists were women, captains' wives who accompanied

234

Preface.

Scripsi in
nave Conteste in annis
MDCCCLXVI, MDCCCLXVII, et MDCCCLXVIII

This journal is being
written on board the ship Contest
and I propose to write in it
an account of the occurrences,
accidents, doings, exploits &c &c
during the present whaling
voyage, especially those in
which "ego ipse" am concerned.

These pages are
written for no one but myself, and if any one should
have the temerity to read thus
far; either from chance, or
evil design, or natural and
inherent depravity; let him
pause ..... and after this solemn
warning if he turns over this
leaf, let it be at his peril;
he has chosen a course that
will inevitably lead him to
———— the end of this book,
if he continues reading long
enough. Therefore I say,
beware my vengeance!

R. G. N. Swift's preface to his journal, kept on board the ship *Contest* of
New Bedford.

their husbands. The earliest of these seafaring women was Mary Hayden Russell of Nantucket, who sailed with Captain Joseph Russell on the *Emily* of London in 1822.[18] Others followed her example, until it was not uncommon for captains' wives to meet at gams. Few of these women attempted much creative writing, although their journals are often filled with florid descriptions of foreign ports and in general make more interesting reading than those of their husbands.[19]

Perhaps the best of the female journalists was Elizabeth Morey. (Her poem on the death of her pet pig appears in chapter III.) Twenty-three years old and just married, Mrs. Morey left Nantucket in 1853 for the first time in her life on a whaling voyage with her husband, Captain Israel Morey of the *Phoenix*. Her journal is filled with naive and personal commentary, sketches, and poetry.[20] Although the journal is in every way a success, she had no high opinion of it herself. Her final entry (she ran out of space August 13, 1855) reads: 'So ends this Book and a Poorley written Volume it is but I have Miereley writen it for my own Amusement.' Besides short occasional verses and sketches, Mrs. Morey's journal records her fanciful names for every whale the *Phoenix* took, such as Jonah, Mercy, The Sea Queen of Russia, Fanny Fern,[21] the Mammoth Cave, Queen Victoria, Prince Albert, Napoleon Boneypart, Josaphene, Queen Caroline, the Russian Ranger, and, less formally, Buster. But Mrs. Morey's journal is atypical. Fresh and untutored, it contains few of the more conventional effusions that lard the journals of most whaling wives.

The whalemen writers were influenced by the literary trends of both England and America. The great era of whaling coincided with the burgeoning of the popular press. It was a time when writing, especially that of poetry, was regarded as an easily cultivated talent. Amateurs, having mastered mechanical rudiments, filled newspapers and magazines with less than third-rate work, most of it pompous, sentimental, and poorly crafted.[22] In the Age of Democracy, the gap between literacy and literary art was considered a narrow one. The published results of this period are predictable: a few very good works, some passable attempts, and reams of some of the worst poetry ever composed in English.[23]

Would-be writers were enticed by the ease and regularity of contemporary literary forms. Songs, poetry, fiction, prose – all were highly standardized, following easily recognized and duplicated models.

AGAIN I AM ON THE DEEP

This was an age fond of singing, in church, in town concerts, or after dinner with friends. At home with the family, singing as entertainment was as common as watching television is today. Common metrical hymn forms dominated both secular song and secular poetry and are standard in the whalemen's journals. Each is basically a four-line stanza. Common meter, or Old English ballad meter, alternates lines of eight and six syllables, and rhymes *abab* or *abcb*. Short meter has lines of six, six, eight, and six syllables, and rhymes *abab* or *abcb*. Long meter has lines of eight syllables each, which may rhyme *abab*, *aabb*, or *abba*. With few variations, these are the forms followed by the whalemen, like most other amateur and professional poets of the time.

The popular fiction of the day – sentimental (and, later, dime) novels and storypaper fiction – was also rigidly patterned. Characters were stereotyped, situations predictable, style universal. In many cases, even the titles were all but identical.[24] Whalemen writers used these patterns too.

The mid-nineteenth century produced vast amounts of cheap, conventional literature, and many whalemen read it.[25] No wonder: in both the cramped quarters of the officers and the squalid quarters of the crew, monotony was ever present. Voyages were long (three years was common), and months could go by without sighting a whale. Shipboard tasks took up part of the day, but still there were long bleak stretches that scrimshawing, singing, and fighting could never fill. For many, reading was the best escape. Francis Olmsted's *Incidents of a Whaling Voyage* (1841) describes a forecastle designed with its crew's literary entertainment in mind.

The forecastle of the North America is much larger than those of most ships of her tonnage, and is scrubbed out regularly every morning. There is a table and a lamp, so that the men have conveniences for reading and writing if they choose to avail themselves of them; and many of them are practising writing every day or learning how to write. Their stationery they purchase out of the ship's stores, and then come to one of the officers or myself for copies, or to have their pens mended. When not otherwise occupied, they draw books from the library in the cabin, and read; or if they do not know how, get someone to teach them. We have a good library on board, consisting of about two hundred volumes . . . .[26]

In the same work, Olmsted states that many other whaleships resembled the *North America*. He was mistaken. Few whaleships had any library at all. Most whalemen were limited to what they brought with them or what they could exchange during gams. J. Ross Browne's *Etchings of a Whaling Cruise* (1846) describes the more usual situation.

As to reading, I was necessarily compelled to read whatever I could get. Unfortunately, I had brought neither books nor papers with me, so that I had to depend entirely on the officers, none of whom were troubled with a literary taste. Mr. D____, the first mate, who was very friendly toward me, had a bundle of old Philadelphia weeklies, which I read over a dozen times, advertisements and all. The cooper, a young man from New Bedford, was by far the most intelligent man aft. His stock of literature consisted of a temperance book, a few Mormon tracts, and Lady Dacre's Diary of a Chaperone . . . . One of my shipmates had a Bible; another, the first volume of Cooper's Pilot; a third, the Songster's own Book; a fourth, the Complete Letter Writer; and a fifth claimed, as his total literary stock, a copy of the Flash newspaper, published in New York . . . . I read and reread all of these. Every week I was obliged to commence on the stale reading, placing the last read away until I systematically arrived at them again . . . .[27]

Until about 1830, a turning point for American literature as well as American whaling, the published authors mentioned or quoted in journals are the traditional British and American favorites still known today. References are frequent to such writings as Shakespeare's plays, the Bible, the poetry of Alexander Pope, James Thomson's 'The Seasons,' and Edward Young's 'Night Thoughts.' After 1830, the rise of the popular press widened the scope of available reading matter and generally lowered its quality. Seven compulsive listmakers, all officers, have left full records of their shipboard reading. The later the list, the more prevalent are ephemera, dime novels or their equivalents. Frederick H. Russell, on the *Pioneer* in the 1870's, lists fifty-nine novels and nine 'Stories I have read in the ledger [clearly a newspaper]' as his reading for that voyage.[28] While he did read such popular and now classic novels as *The Black Tulip*, *The Woman in White*, *Oliver Twist*, and *Our Mutual Friend*, most of Russell's list is comprised of sensational literature. At least eight entries are from

AGAIN I AM ON THE DEEP

Beadle's series of dime novels, and many have titles like *Adelaide the Avenger* and *Chenga the Cheyenne*.

Russell's journal includes his contributions to a pornographic ballad, which he seems to have written in collaboration with a fellow crewman. But such creative efforts were rare by the 1870's. Whaling journals became more and more perfunctory; even official logbooks were often penciled in irregular scrawls. The industry, as well as the education and character of the men engaged in it, rapidly deteriorated.

The following chapters include selections from the work of forty-two whalemen of whaling's golden age whose writing followed, occasionally surpassed, and sometimes even cleverly parodied the conventions of the time. Although some examples are from the forecastle, a majority of these journalists are officers, and, most often, captains. Three prolific writers stand out: Captains Samuel Braley and Ambrose Bates, and mate George Mills. Only a fraction of their work appears here, but that fraction represents their broad range of topics and of literary forms.

The selections are arranged topically, according to the themes that preoccupied whalemen. These range from occasional musings about home to the writers' most important preoccupation: whaling itself.

CHAPTER TWO

MY THOUGHTS ON HOME
DO DWELL

Whalemen devoted a great deal of space in their journals to thoughts of the homes and families they left behind. Homesickness afflicted seasoned officers and green hands alike. With the sinking of land below the horizon on the journey out, as several outward-bound journalists comment, came the sinking of the heart.

Most thoughts of home written in journals followed current convention and were sometimes so cliché-ridden and general as to be meaningless. Some writers did record their memories of home more individually and experimentally. These journalists were usually the most prolific; some could pursue almost any subject, no matter how disturbing. However, more often the writers clung to convention, perhaps as a way of avoiding specific – and thus painful – remembrances.

William Stimpson's 'Home,' for example, is clearly the product of much thought. He revised his draft several times, then made a fair copy. His essay echoes one of the most famous songs of the period, 'Home! Sweet Home!,' which had been sung throughout England and America since the 1820's. But Stimpson's prose carries these simple sentiments a little further than the song. Although many of his comments are based on his own experience, his closing reference to 'splendor and gaiety in all its formes' is quite unlike his other journal descriptions of life at sea. It is, perhaps, wish-fulfillment.

Home

How many sweet endearing ties lie centered there. I care not Weather I be a native of one of the far distant isles of the Pacific or of the greatest metropilis of the Union When a Wanderer from home his happiest moments are passed in meditating on the place of his youthfull abode. friends Kindred and every thing pertaining to happiness encircled there pleasure gaity and happiness are

*to be found elsewhere but Still When amidst all these there is something Which
calls our Memory back to Youthfull scnes And we meditate upon the Spot
with feelings of pleasure and happiness and we live in expectation and hopes of
visiting it again and When returning to the spot all our thoughts Are absorbed
in the contemplation of Wandering around and mingling With those Which
were our companions in Youth and viewing the scens of our childhood, I care
not Wether home be ever so Meek and lowly it has enticements there Whch are
not to be elsewhere enjoyed though We Wander among splendor and gaiety in
all its formes*[1]

A song by George Mills, an officer on the *Mary Frances* in 1856, is much
more specific in its details, as in his use of his own first name. Although
the clichés of home are still present – sometimes as comically distorted as
the dome-shaped chimneys – the song happily concentrates on the joys of
affection that await his return.

Song By G. E. Mills. We Come. we come

We come – we come. in joy to greet you
Sweet dear old home so kind and true
Endeared by youthfull reccollections
In you I find there's nothing new.
I long to see thy chimneys rising.
Like unto some Lofty dome
And the shouts of welcome – welcome.
From dear Friends thats now at home.

My absence seems of long duration
Since that parted we have been
Yet thy Joys are ne're forgotten.
Though through gilded halls I've been
Brighter. fairer – Choicer Flowers –
Yet where e're my footsteps roam
I can never bring my mind
To forget the Joys of home

The allurements of fairer nations
Held out attractions unto me
Yet I left them all forever.

Denied them all sweet home for thee.
Not many days shall pass around
Before our footsteps turn thy way
And there amidst thy best affections
I hope I ne're shall want to stray.

Then – Ho – for home. we come – we come
With Glad hearts warmly burning
With thoughts that roam towards far off home
To which were fast returning
And as we gather 'round the spot
To me the Sound – George – welcome
I answer to the Joyous shout
We come – Sweet Friends – We come[2]

Mills's hope that he would never 'want to stray' was shared by most career whalemen. Many other journals describe happy arrivals at home that soon give way to bouts of boredom and restlessness, driving the sailor back to sea. Once on board, waving farewell, these whalemen generally found the whole cycle in motion once more, and began longing for home, berating themselves for misusing time on shore.

Another songwriter, Samuel G. Swain of Nantucket, combines his thoughts of home with a general record of the voyage so far. His 'Song Composed on Thoughts of Home' belies its title somewhat. While it voices conventional sorrows, for Swain home means little more than a brief stopover, then 'off to Sea for More.'

Swain's references to the scarcity of whales come from the period when whaleships were forced to sail further and further north in their search, and whalemen became some of the most important sea explorers of their time. His comments on money are also pertinent. Whalemen were not paid a fixed salary, but were assigned shares of a ship's profits according to rank. Some whalemen's compensations equaled or bettered those on shore. But when a cruise was unsuccessful, all hands suffered. At times, a whaleman might earn no more from a three-year voyage than could support a spree or two at home. Some even arrived home in debt to the ship's slop chest.

Swain's song was 'composed . . . Nov 24 Of. the island of New Zealand while in bad weather Laying to in & heavy gale of wind.' Stephen Easton,

Jr., in whose journal Swain recorded his song, adds a confused though heartfelt chorus.

Song Composed on Thoughts of Home

Loud howls the winds
The billows roars
My thoughts on home does dwell
Of happy Scenes thats past and gone
With them i love So well

2

Dear friends its hard the Seas to rove
No hardships can compare
Through Storms and calms wer tossed about
With hearts worn out with cares

3

From place to place we Shift about
In hopes Some whales to See
But times has altered verry fast
All on the Stormy Seas

4

The whales ar Scarce the times nears long
To what it used to be
So Many Ships & cruising round
But whales they canot See

5

Its now we r on the Southern ground
New Zyelands Stormy Coast
The gales blows hard our Ship hove to
Small chance their is for fish

6

These are the times that makes us Sad
While we are on cruising ground
What can we do but Sigh and Say
We wish we wer at home

7

But what can a Sailor do at home
What pleasures can he See
Unless he has his pockets lined
With what he s earned at Sea

8

Money is the bane of all our thoughts
Whitch makes go from the
So far away from you me love
To cross the Stormy Seas

9

Kind fortune might come to us yet
Although we ve had no luck
Its not to late we do not mourn
Our voayge is but half up

10

Eighteen long months has past and gone
Since we have left our isle
Five and twenty more
Wee ll come on Shore
On old Nantucket isle

11

And when we do return again
Short Stay we ll make on Shore
We ll have our Spree and then make Sail
And off to Sea for More

Chorus——Oh whaling is a ____ hard trade
And I have found it out
And if ever I get home again
Ill keep a Sharp lookout – for a spirm[3]

J. Goram composed two songs about his native Nantucket: 'Bound Home' and 'We ll soon be ther.' The first recounts an eventful voyage, including storms, cannibalism, and paganism, and concludes with the joys of home and friends. Goram's verses are smoother than most, and the sentiments, though conventional, are carefully organized. As a cooper, Goram was probably better educated than many of the crew.

Bound Home

Our Ship no longer braves the seas
But safely in the haven rests
Old oceans storms and tempests cease
And frendships arms are round and pressed

O'er many a weary mile weve sped
On foreign shores we have often stood
Where man oh! fellow man hath fed
And sacraficed with human blood

Where heathen nations bow the bow
To idol gods of wood and stone
In lands where Milk and honey flowed
But heavens Creator is unknown

In deadly strife we oft have stood
With huge Leviathan oceans pride
His giant strength gaints Skill have placed
And left his Corse upon the tide

But now through dangers safely passed
Again we tread our native shore
Joy fills our bosoms unsurpassed
To vew our home and friends once more

Again we vew each well Known scene
Familiar forms now meet our eye
On every face beams joy Serene
And sorrowing bosoms cease to sigh

To Chide our hopes and raise our fears
Cold winter now may strive in vain
Comfort with outspread arms appears
Repays the dangers of the Main[4]

MY THOUGHTS ON HOME DO DWELL

Goram wrote his second song just a few miles from port, off 'gay Head under storm sails.' This song is more joyful than 'Bound Home.' Near shore, Goram could more readily imagine his homecoming, and he conjures up vivid memories – particularly of the Yankee girls.

We ll soon be there

> *Hurah! hurrah! were homeward bound*
> *Hurrah the wind blowes fair*
> *With joy let every bosom bound*
> *Well soon, well soon be there*
>
> *Haul line Haul line ye Yankee girls*
> *And coil it clean and fair*
> *Then rig ye out with rings and curls*
> *Well soon well soon be there*
>
> *O mind ye not what landsmen say*
> *The storm they fear to dare*
> *They'll skulk like beaten dogs away*
> *Well soon well soon be there*
>
> *Hurrah! we smell the Yankee sod*
> *Haul line nor slack a hair*
> *Though rain pours down like old Noahs flood*
> *Well son well soon be there*
>
> *And ye who wish to be a bride*
> *If ye are paſsing fair*
> *Haul line and with the wind and tide*
> *Well soon well soon be there*
>
> *Hurrah! Hurrah a few leagues more*
> *Well throw aside all care*
> *Then with the handsome girls on shore*
> *Well son well soon be there*[5]

Hiram King's 'hone sweet hone how I love you' is as unskilled a poem as any in the journals, but his sadness and longing are emotionally convincing.

hone sweet hone how I love you
though far a way from the I roam
and if I ever do forgit the
it will bea when I lay in the tune [tomb]

ofer my Hone far of the Ocean
i still Shal think of hone
tine will not alter my deviton [devotion]
nor change the thought of such as nee [me]

sone may think Well or franket
for writing such lines as these
i an shure my pen is not growing antic
to striving ny her mind to please

my mother Dear i will not for git you
Brothers and sisters still the sane
With me as when first I left you
to cruse upon the raging main

My others freinds do ne renbember
When I an far a way
i will prove trew to ther novain [?] assenbley
ny mind never shal never fron the stray

But now i will stop riting
or elce I shall turn crazy
and if i do it will be when
I an taking sick or lazy [.] x orginal H R
King on boart of the barck fortune[6]

In 1850 Captain Samuel T. Braley, one of the most prolific of all the
whalemen journalists, returned again and again to thoughts of home.
Sometimes he toyed with what he knew to be mechanical and conventional verse. In the margin of his journal, beside the poem about home that
follows, he comments, 'cant write any more such poetry as this it will not
pay for the space it ocupies in my book.'

We have had good wind now for 2 days and I feal in rather better spirrits and I am agoing to try my poetry machine but you will find it rather out of tune – but "here goes"

> *As o'er the bosom of the Sea,*
> *With almost concious pride;*
> *My bonny Bark is bounding free,*
> *And flings the spray aside.*
> *With grief I view her fleet carear,*
> *While dashing through the foam,*
> *She bears me still from all that's dear,*
> *My much regreted home.*
>
> *And dearly do I love that home;*
> *Though now so far away,*
> *That I am in another zone,*
> *And changed the night to day:*
> *The chords that bind me to that spot,*
> *Will sever but with life;*
> *Thy hallowed name is n'er forgot*
> *My own, my darling Wife.*[7]

Braley's 'machine' also turned out some quite extraordinary pieces. A journal entry of 31 December 1849 tells how a whaleman could feel more fearful than joyous when he finally did return from a long voyage. At sea, communication with home was irregular at best, with ships bearing letters to whalemen with addresses no more exact than 'the Pacific Ocean.' Many letters never reached their destination as ships crisscrossed the seas. As a result, a whaleman's return home often meant painful news of deaths, as well as happy encounters with toddlers who had been unborn when father left.

Samuel Braley's romantic recollections of a reunion with his young wife are as tender and loving as the references to her in general throughout his journals.

The last year is one above all others of my life of 32 years in which I must look back upon for a few momints On the first of last January I was off the Island of Ceylon looking for whales, and soon after was obliged to leave for home, having tryed in vain to get more provision in order to lengthen my voyage and I started with a heavy heart expecting to meet nothing but cold looks from my owners and to find her whome I had long cherrished as the Idol of my heart numbered with the dead; not having heared a word from her during the whole time of my long stay; and under those circumstances it is not strange if the homeward passage was rather unpleasent, but long looked for, though dreded moment at lengt arrived we cast our anchor in the harbour of New Bedford, and although it was mid-night I hastened on shore, determined to know the worst as soon as posible when I landed I found the streets deserted save now and the a solitery watchman, I found my way to a livery stable and after much ado I got the hostler up and after making dew enquireys who I was he harnesed me a horse and I starteg to find some one that could tell me something about my wife I drove accross the bridge and went to the residence of Capt Cox, and after much ringing and pounding I turned him out he came to, and raised an upper front window and enquired who was thare I told him where is the Ship? I told him she was lying at Clarks point with 1800 bbls of sperm oil in her said he you have done well Braley that gave me much incouragement I asked him if he could give me any information conserning my wife yes said I guess so ah thought I she is not dead then Mrs Cox came them and said that she saw her a short time before and she was then in very good health although she had been very sick the last summer. I then felt satisfied, my mind was at rest, on the two most important subjects that had ingrossed it for two years, I felt as though I could sit down in the middle of the road and sit till day light but then I thought I mite as well go on, so I started; It was a fine summers morning and I enjoyed the ride very much every thing was quiet, and as I past objects that were familiar to me, I thought how little they had changed in the course of three years and a half. at length after an hour and a halfs drive I reached the dwelling of that being most dear to me on earth I drove up to the gate, quietly hitched my horse, and went to the doar how my heart beet but as I knocked, and knocked again before I awoke any one of the household, at last I heard a moove within and a voice asking who is there which I knew to belong to the Father of my wife; I replied, a friend; and he opened the doar; I entered and seated myself without serrimony while he went to get a light and to call Marry Ann who had not awoke by all the nois that had been made but after calling her two or three times he made her understan that I had come, and then he came back with a light, and sat down to have a yarn, but what he said I know

*not for my eyes were fixed on her chair that I knew she had ocupied the
evening before and my thoughts were with her that I heard in another room;
how I wished that he would go but he seamed not to notice my uneasiness and
sat still, for how long I know not but it seamed to me an age and I was on the
point of asking for Mary Ann a second time, whin he took the hint and started,
then my heart jumped up in my throat and I could hardly breath but the long
looked for moment came at last and she entered the room and losed the door,
I flew to her caught her in my arms, I gased into her face and insted of finding
the raviges of the iron hand of desease I beheld the smile of health and youthfull beauty which excelled any thing I had ever seen in that face before, and
above all it was lit up with the blush of maiden modisty that would hardly
permit her to wellcom her wanderer back; but oh that kiss! from those sweet
lips that were pressed in fondness to mine; it went to my fingersends, and told
me in plainest turms how much I was beloved by that little heart that I felt
flutter so plainly shall I ever forget it? yes, when I forget to breath It was the
happiest moment of my life. From that time till I sailed on this voyage I was
like a devotee at the shrine of his God, happy nowhare but there, and there
supremly so*

*That time I would wish to live over again and it is the only period in my
life that I can say the same of.; but the end came as must allways be with
human happiness, but it was hard to part, the hardest tryal that ever was laid
on me and if I am spared to meet her again nothing shall part us but the fear
of starving so has passed the year, how the next one will pass is unknown but
at all events I shall not see my wife, nor the next, nor the next but I hope the
time will come that I shall again be happy But I am affraid that I place to
much of my affections on her and not enough on Him who gave her to me, but
I will try to do both*

*I am now farely started on a long and tedious voyage and whin I look
forward upon it my heart sinks to think of the tryals that mist be contended
with and obstickles that must be overcome in order to obtain a cargo; but I
must not anticipate o "suffitiant unto the day is the evle thereof" but will look
forward with Hope and apply myself to the task that is before me with
renewed vigor and humbly trust to the Wise Desposer of events to crown
my efforts with success*

Good night Sweet.[8]

Despite such heartfelt longing for home and loved ones as Braley and the others describe, most whalemen could never reconcile the contrary attractions of sea and shore. Few writers mention the problem in their creative work, but complaints show up often in daily journal entries. A common aspect of the whaleman's character seems to have been chronic dissatisfaction with the current situation, be it ship or shore, and a desire to be somewhere else.

Ambrose Bates, one of the more industrious writers, explored this ambivalence in a poem and an essay. His poem 'May 1867' describes one of its more common manifestations, the distorted sense of the passage of time that disturbed many whalemen during shore leaves.

May 1867

And I have stood and time has brought
Me back unto old ocean's gloom
My carless brain ne'er lent one thought
Of how much I should miss my home
 Twas when I had but four weeks grace
 To stay at home. I did not haste
But thoughtless said that four weeks more
Was very long and I would be
Already then if not before.
So one week passed and there was three
 Somehow it seemed that week had gone
 Too soon. The next would tarry long
But crossgrained time had spread his wing
And quick the moments flew away
I saw at last it soon must bring
The morning of a parting day
 Which long upon my heart would leave
 A pang which silently must grieve
And then I saw a few short days
Remaining. They had precious grown
Whilst through my brain a thousand ways
Were marked that I might yet prolong
 Their number which were less'ning fast
 As one by one went stealing past

MY THOUGHTS ON HOME DO DWELL

At last I saw the close of day
The sun in glowing beams go down
The last till months must pass away
In times steady but lazing round
  One night remained. No pillowed rest
  Could make me dream that I was blest
Unwelcome morn and thou art here
Yet the rabble of the world goes on
Friends too are near me But the cheer
Of happiness Alas is gone
  And floating o'er the morbid bay
  The signal calls I must away
And leave with you my native land
Hopes which But life time could unfold
Reluctant now I clasp the hand
E'er long I'd give a world to hold
  I meet a glance though dimed with tears
  Will follow me through long absent years
Now oft I turn to shun the thought
The pang it brings, the pang it brought
Oh could I wash in Lethe's stream
From memory that recuring dream
To muse o'er childhoods gentle shade
And happy scenes which time betrayed
Twould help to soothe a drooping mind
And fancies borrowed sun to shine[9]

A month later, in 'June 1867,' Bates expressed the same thoughts in a more personal style. Bates's 'truant heart' again leads him back to the sea, away from home, but 'the traitor wave' offers no lasting satisfaction.

June 1867
Over and over again and I do not know but it always will be my lot to live in uneasiness In vain I have sough a place upon this globe that I might settle down in quite contentment But alas none has yet lured me from this wild inclination for roaming And although I have been blessed with all the heart could ask still as it seems almost against my will I find myself vointeerly flying from all I love on earth

In former times I used to say and believe that I with one to share my fortunes I could quietly spend my days in some humble cot from the tumult of the world But time passed and that one I found to my minutest satisfaction And all that I had ever dreamed or wished for was mine. Virtue Truth beauty and evry quality that ever was deemed good was combined in one person. And that person was given me to cheer and make me that home that I had so often wished for

And so I laid down my traveling armor and bid old time to roll and I would dream out my remaining days in my happy home

I was happy But I often found my truant heart sighing for those wild scenes of excitement which so long before had surrounded me. But still I did not dream that anything could induce me to cherish one single Idea of leaveing my newly found joyes for all the world contained beside

But instead of finding my roaming inclinations relaxing each day found a new plea for my old pastime And e'er long I found myself anticipating a voyage to sea. I sailed but as the last hill went beneath the horison I found instead of contentment that I was the most unhappy mortal liveing. And many was the long month I fased waiting and longing to return to those joyes I had forsaken

I returned I was happy and hard as it had been for me to leave those I loved and although those long dreary months were fresh in my memory yet still I find myself again about my old haunts, habits, and longings for the devil knows what.

Though I eaver dreaded the hour that I should say good bye to her my idol Still I went and still I repented. Again I am here a lonely lonely man. If I was a drinking man I would curs the bowl. If I was a fool it would make but little differance whire I was. But am I the only one that is grieving through these long long days

> *Tis her I love the best of all*
> *Who is sad I fear me*
> *Whilst here I roam from spring to fall*
> *Oer the ocean weary*
> *Though oft as now Ive pledeged before*
> *To ride the traitor wave no more*
> *From her I love most dearly*
> *That parting hour clings to my soul*
> *Still sadning in its onward roll*[10]

MY THOUGHTS ON HOME DO DWELL

Franklin Tobey, second mate on the *Atlantic* in 1846, wrote a rather odd poem about leaving home. It begins conventionally enough, describing a tearful ride with a sweetheart to a picnic the day before the narrator will ship out on another whaling voyage. But when the couple arrives at the grove, the scene becomes surreal: the clams and oysters boiling in the chowder scream and bawl, even more openly mournful in their fate than the narrator is in his. He recognizes the similarity: 'like me they were filled with Deep sorrow / For then they were there / But they couldnot tell where / Their Companions would be on the morrow / ... And like me they Crys / O spare me the pain of tomorrow.' The comparison is deliberate, and the effect is comic. Is this poem meant to parody the elegiac tradition of all earth's mourning a loss? Or is it simply a sarcastic flight of fancy? In any case, Tobey's bizarre version of a scene most whalemen took seriously is a surprise.

> the morning was damp and the sky was orecast
> And the sun was hid from my sight
> My thoughts they were sad for the Day was the last
> That I should spend with the girl of my own Hearts delight
>
> And it filled my mind with deep sorrow
> For a Letter I had received
> Which caused me to grieve
> For it told me I must leave my Dear girl on the morrow
>
> But the sun shone out bright and the Clouds wore away
> And the Day prooved pleasant and fair
> Yet I knew but to well twas the very last Day
> For many long years that I should spend there
> And it filled my mind with Deep sorrow
> For my Heart was not there
> Twas almost in Dispair
> As I bitterly though of the morrow
>
> But twas no use to repine at what I could not help
> So I harnessed my old Horse to the waggon
> And went after the girls like any young Whelp
> And Drove Like a furious Draggon

AND THE WHALE IS OURS

To Drive from my mind that Deep sorrow
I talked all I could
But stay there it would
For I had to leave my Dear girl on the morrow

It was the fourth of July as togather we Drove
And the Birds were singing quite cheerely
I was bound for the PicNic all in the green grove
With the girl that I loved most Dearly
Yet my mind it was filled with Deep sorrow
For she kept a crying
And I kept a sighing
At the thoughts of leaveing my Dear on the morrow

When we came to the Grove all in the green wood
There were faces both pretty and smileing
And round a large Fire a great many stood
Watching the Pot in which the Chouder was boiling
But the Clams they were filled with deep sorrow
At the Thoughts of being scalled
so they screamed and they bawled
We shall be eaten before this time tomorrow

They Oysters looked on at the great prepareations
And they opened thier shells and they hooped
Pray dont commit such sad depredations
For we do not wish to be souped
And like me they were filled with Deep sorrow
For then they were there
But they couldnot tell where
Their Companions would be on the morrow

But the Cook paid no attention to Oysters or Clams
At least unto what they were saying
But into their mouth a large knife he crams
And immediately commences their slaying
Twas then that their shells burst with sorrow

Tears filled their Eyes
And like me they Crys
O spare me the pain of tomorrow

The water we Drank was from a large Pond
In which the young Urchins were swiming
We made Lemonade of which they were fond
And the Girls like to have their glasses filled briming
But in my glass was a drop of Deep sorrow
For instead of Lemonade
I was afraid
I should drink nothing but Tears on the morrow [11]

Two writers already discussed, George Mills and Ambrose Bates, made shore life the basis for much longer and more ambitious works. Neither effort is specifically about the author's own home; both are melodramatic.

'The Grandfathers Story' is Bates's most ambitious work, a narrative poem of nearly eighty stanzas with nine lines each. The poem takes up the more popular themes of Victorian melodrama. In fact, the story could easily be illustrated with a series of such Currier & Ives prints as 'The Mother's Death,' 'The Friendless Boy,' and 'Young Love.'

The grandfather is an old man named Charley who tells his life story. As a child, he tries hard to please, but his father inexplicably hates the boy. Charley's efforts are futile: his cruel father 'feast[s] his eyes on infants tears.' After Charley's mother dies, the child wanders forlornly until taken in by the motherly wife of a sailor. Charley has lost a mother, she a son; when her husband returns, the family is complete. Charley grows up and he too goes to sea. He returns from a successful voyage to find a daughter, Annie, has been born to his adopted family. Charley rejoices with his foster parents, then returns to sea with his foster father, only to face countless hazards in the course of which the foster father is drowned with all the crew but Charley. Luckily, a smuggler's ship rescues Charley and he joins the crew. Finally Charley returns home to save his foster mother and Annie from poverty. He marries Annie (although according to the chronology of the poem she is a child of about eleven or so), and they have a daughter who dies after giving birth to her own daughter. In his old age, Charley narrates his story to his young granddaughter.

The poem is a success story, a sailor's rags-to-riches tale, in emotional as well as material terms, and there is certainly action enough for any swashbuckler. The scene of the friendless 'orphan' at the cottage gate, which is the focus of most of the repetition, was one which appeared in many contemporary prints and engravings, as well as in popular songs such as Mrs. Opie's 'The Orphan Boy's Tale.'

Not all of the poem is convention-ridden. For example, the stanza describing Charley's sickness on his first voyage has vivid detail, and the simile portraying his recovery, when he 'hove ahead like Jonah's whale,' is undoubtedly Bates's own. 'Annie,' we find from reading Bates's journal, was the name of his own sweetheart.

The Grandfathers Story

One Autumn month I took my gun
And hied me for a day of chance
Among the fethered fowls that swum
O'er the millpond in negligance
And there I lingered though the sun
Anounced that day was shurely done
And twilight marching in advance
Left me with night too long before
I reached my distant cottage door

My path led near a mansion bold
And o'er it waved some stately trees
I paused one moment to behold
The moon-beams danceing through their leaves
A merry voice broke on my ear
So sweet so plaintive and so near
I durst not stir nor hardly breathe
And there I heard a tale of strife
Of love of hope a checkered life

Beneath those trees the shadows sweet
Whire playes the Zephyrs of the night
Natures are [?] Angels guarding sleep
So listless in their mild delight

MY THOUGHTS ON HOME DO DWELL

And here a sound my ear decoys
Me thought to sweet for human voice
Though near nights mantle mocked my sight
It said grandfather. will you pleas
Tell a story – I will not teas

An old man said my Darling child
So long ago as I am old
There was a boy though gay and wild
He nevertheless was kind and bold
His rogueish ways did not escape
The vengence of a fathers hate
Which in this tale shall not be told.
I would not that thy guiless heart
Were wounded with the cruel part

He had Brothers and sisters too
I wish that you had Emma dear
But this chill and falling dew
Is gathering fast upon us here
It is not wisdom then to stay
And sow the seed of lifes decay
Whire hopelessness might laugh at fear
And though I braved. through lifes long blast
Of all my hopes, you are the last

That father by a blazeing fire
Sat in his easy chair one night
The little ones did all aspire
To win a favor in his sight
And all succeeded well, but one
And him of cours the rest must shun
Though he had strove with all his might
To be as good and loved as they
Was scorned and driven from the play

His little hopes would oft revive
In dreams of sunny days to come

His mother then was still alive
The only friend he yet had known
And when the fathers angry voice
Forbade his young heart to rejoice
He sought his mother She alone
Could bid his throbing heart be still
In soothing accents to her will

When he was born his Father gave
The name of Charles unto his son
A name from o'er a dear friends grave
Whome he wished to honor and mourn
But since had learned to hate that name
A Father. What man could do the same
And hate a child. Much more his own
To vent his hate in low mean snears
And feast his eyes on infants tears

No tongue can tell no pen can mark
One shadow of that helpless gloom
Which saw that mothers form depart
Forever to the silent tomb
The smothered anguish of his grief
Unsympathized might seek relief
And only find himself alone
With selfish world all spread before
Behind had envy closed the door

Keen blew the wind o'er wood and plain
Rolled in the distant Autumns sun
Strugling onward as though it fain
Would end the circuit there begun
In yellow robes the trees were bowed
As mourning summer in a shroud
Whose rosy fields the frost had stung
And left them withering black and bare
For winters self would soon be there

MY THOUGHTS ON HOME DO DWELL

On such a morn there might been seen
A homeless boy with naked feet
With cotton shirt and trouses thin
Whire want might boast herself compleet
A Stranger in a stranger land
A Lad like this could not command
A place among the clean and neat
Whilst oft his little heart would fail
As oft ambition would prevail

He paused before a rural gate
Which opened toward a cottage home
A Lady smileing did not wait
For words, his hopelessness to own
But bade him in to rest and warm
And asked him wheather he was going
So lightly clad and yet alone
And Charley said to find a friend
My future shall be a reckomend

This Lady was a sailors wife
Her husband then upon the sea
Whire he had passed most of his life
Relenting in his harsh decree
The little months he knew at home
Were joyes which are only known
Expectant through adversity
And with indulgance strove to pay
The helpless doubts of far away

Yes evry pleasure that the mind
With brain and study could invent
What Love and wealth might help to find
The past and present to content
Were gathered round their happy board
Joyes of a two years hoard
And friends around had also lent

Their own goodwill A cheerful voice
With the joyful to rejoice

And when this wandering boy become
A supliant before her gate
She bade the little stranger name
The reason why so cold and late
So thinly clad and yet alone
In stranger land and there unknown,
Then Charley ventured to relate
His mothers death. How all beside
To cheer the orphan was denied

And then she told him he should be
Her little boy and have a home
That some day he might live to see
Whirein God blessed him thus to roam
And then she dressed him neat and warm
In clothes her own little boy had worn
For she had lost a little son
And Charles now should eaven fil
The lonely place he left so still

The sailor from the southern sea
Browned beneath a tropic sun
Once more returns. How glad is he
To find and bless the absent one
And Charley hailed the joyful day
And tried to be as glad as they
Here let me tell how they become
To be great friends. And mammoth scheems
Came into being through Charleys dreams

But leaveing such childish notions
And those early dreams of pleasure
Whilst the Captain returns unto the ocean
To meet the fair and stormy weather

MY THOUGHTS ON HOME DO DWELL

Here Charley saw with heavy heart
His friend and noble ship depart
Which left him scheeming at his leasure
How someday he would plow the wave
And be a sailor just as brave

The next two years he went to school
And followed on in wisdoms train
Conquering problems Minding rules
But still his fancy sought the main
And evry thought he did possess
But aded to that one distress
But here the Captain comes again
Then silent tears were hid away
For life had blessed another day

Those lonely hours dull time had chased
Now seem to mount some fleeting wing
And onward rolled the car apace
Which soon the parting hour will bring
And Charley joyed as day by day
Time hastened on and fled away
And he forgot each liveing thing
That he had loved Since he should be
A sailor now. So glad was he

From Boston harbor down the tide
With bounceing breeze A Ship had sailed
The noblest of all. The rovers Bride
Where art o'er nature had prevailed
On her deck stood our sailor boy
For the mate had piped all hands ahoy
No favorite there could be detailed
Each man must know his place to fill
To come or go To anothers will

The ship began to pitch and roll
Some dam their eyes and some their luck

The iner man. brooks not controll
Whilst liver and all seems comeing up
Sea legs are missing Charley rolled
When he could not crawl hold by hold
At last he reached the water but
And swallowed once of Adams ale
Then hove ahead like Jonah's whale

And then he wished he was at home
The sailors life might go to pot
He never again would think to roam
So very bold when he was not
Twas very fine to talk and read
But this was misory indeed
And verified upon the spot
But then he said I'll whine no more
Since yet I see my native shore

And he conquored though the task
Was sick and sore. Yet well he knew
Those ills could not forever last
Therefore he tried to rush them through
So straightened up. Put on a look
That spoke in volumes. And he took
His fate so quiet that it drew
The approbation of men and mate
Who reconciled him to his fate

For ten long months this noble ship
Had [?] they o'er the trackless main
Oft Charley saw the bright sun dip
Far down o'er the watery plain
And he had seen far Indies shore
But now ill seek his home once more
Right joyful to return again
Now the high hill lifts in the sky
Then onward. They are drawing nigh

MY THOUGHTS ON HOME DO DWELL

In Boston at Commercial dock
As swan like The Rovers Bride
Magesticaly rides upon the spot
From whence it ventured on the tide
The Captain already seeks that home
Which seeming long had been alone
But a girl Baby so long denied
Was there. So he forgot to ask
Or tell or care what els had passed

Another came. and on the door
A little rap though very low
And Charley stood upon the floor
Happier than the sunbeams glow
And when his mistress holds his hand
And calls him an adventerous man
That on the ocean should boldly go
He felt that he had conquered all
With her approval none could fall

But Charleys eyes were opened wide
There sat a babe on the old mans knee
He wondered when the little thing cried
Whose noisy stripling it could be
The Lady said come here and view
A little sister which I give to you
Some day perhaps to be your bride
Its name is Annie You must call
It Sister Annie and pleas us all

Domestic sunshine which peeps between
Succeeding voyages on the sea
Are golden moments which intervene
As post-orbits in lifes destory
Whire we may rest the mind from care
As all we love on earth is there
The task is o'er The bond is free

[45]

But Alas that glorious day
Grows brighter but to pass away

Time dashes on. Again they went
In the Rovers Bride as done before
But now some gloom or discontent
Each silent face was shadowing o'er
Some evil or forebodeing fear
On evry thought seemed lurking near
A death grave in the tempests roar
As in the silence of the deep
Some hiden secret it must keep

Let Fancy paint her glowing scenes
For the deluded to admire
Though beauty from those glowing dreams
Will from the sober thought retire
And leave the wandering mind to ask
Of things forgatten in the past
Whire memory still retains desire
Who in confusion must repair
Disgusted from vanities fair

But now behold the truly worth
A ship upon the dark blue sea
The one great beauty which the earth
Reflects her wonder unto me
Her towering mast her snow white sail
When proudly booming through the gale
High o'er the wild vast gay and free
Like pack hounds scenting o'er the plain
Leaps on the rover of the main

With L[?]amper taught and canvass new
The Rovers Bride went down the bay
Friends had watched her as she grew
Less and less in the far away

MY THOUGHTS ON HOME DO DWELL

Again to Indie they are bound
Returning in lifes steady round
To reap new joyes from another day
Although between the cup and lip
Some one has said beware the slip

With gentle breeze and flowing sheet
Far o'er the waters they are bourn
And such the sorrow they shall meet
Who wander from the loved and home
Stil hopeful promises they have found
In joyeous dreams of homeward bound
For men may hope through the unknown
Expectant of life's slow decay
Still on the morrow pass away

Now onward onward as they dash
When the mad waters in the trail
With steady roar and sparkling flash
Phosphoric blaze in Eastern gale
Behold a sound A clash tis past
The Rovers Bride with soul and mast
Has left but one to tell the tale
A Stranger ship had seen them down
When scarce the ear had caught the sound

The ship was struck once long before
The first surprise had passed away
The Bride had sank to rise no more
One moment still. The waters play
O'er sailor and the sailors pride
Whire is their grave O silent tide
Is this the secret Judgment day
Or was it Lethes darkened stream
Which closed above hopes promised dream

The Captain in his birth asleep
Could scarce recall his scattered thoughts

From the first shock. When lo the deep
Had wraped her mantle o'er his corps
If one remaining thought was known
Twas spent in memory of his home
What anguish must that moment brought
One tender dream A wild despair
Upon the instant settled there

In the tumult Charles we find
Safte upon the Strangers deck
Mourning for those he left behind
To perish in the sunken wreck
The stranger ship now backed her sail
And launched the long boat o'er the rail
Fate was decreed. The seal was set
Whilst men shall streach his had to save
Fate points in silence to a grave

They came on board and filled away
Bound off to Chinies distant shore
The deed was done. What boots to stay
To search the silent waters o'er
How Charley escaped the sinking wreck
And climed on board the strangers deck
And how his soul was sick and sore
To know his friends and ship were lost
Are wonders in themselves almost

Now onward as though naught was done
To break upon the steady sound
Which makes the days seem all as one
Whirein no changes can be found
And Charley now the choice shall make
To join the stranger ship or wate
To find another homeward bound
And he accepts as boatswains mate
To share their gain or changeful fate

This noble ship. Stag Hound by name
Was on a voyage of speculation
She had acquired glorious fame
Through the rounds of all creation
But now a smuglar she shall be
And stroll about the China sea
Each man to share his well earned portion
Charley recalled the famous stories
He had read of Smuglars glories

Here let me jump from year to year
From scene to scene whire changes bring
To Charley in his wild career
As bourn on fortunes buoyant wing
Into Hong Kong the Stag Hound came
In ballace there and sailed the same
The crew is posted so they fling
Away ballace. Nor ask if right
To take in opium at night

And so the run from port to port
Changeing cargo when sun and moon
Had other business to report
Which dated from another zone
But one time somebody smelt a mice
When such a ship should come for rice
And things seemed geting in so soon
They up anchor to slip the bay
But found a cutter in the way

Now there was no time to ponder
Fight they must or wear the chain
Fight for freedom. Not to plunder
But to secure themselves and gain
Each man on deck was at his post
And in himself could count a host
While content throbees in evry vain

They felt that theirs was shurely right
So all was risked upon their might

The fight began twas short and sweet
That is – Sweet for the conqueror
For what remains from a defeat
Feels differant from the vanquished there
The Stag Hounds fought for lif and death
They conquered What of them was left
The Captain Their noble lader
With all his mates can do no more
For all are lifeless in their gore

A half wrecked ship without command
The needs repair They must have rest
To veer away for Nomans land
They all agreed was for the best
Along the Lorchoo they must range
Whire the air is cool. The change
Is what they need A tropic blast
Had long been pouring on their brain
Unshaded there might loll in vain

And here upon this ocean Isle
They did disband their little crew
To rest their cair and limbs awhile
And then to form themselves anew
The Stag Hound wrecked from end to end
Some must hew while others shall mend
And all things soon were looking new
Each heart now panted for the sea
To wander o'er the waters free

And so a day was set to sail
But none aspired to the command
Lest he that should and after fail

No inexperience would ever stand
For his excuse with those allied
Nor eaven with the world beside
If ruin come to that dauntless band
Come up and from the dream awake
Risk all when glory is at stake

So they in due time did elect
Young Charley to the chief command
He though reluctant did accept
At last to lead the little band
Nor eighteen summers he had seen
And was a boy just in his teens
But yet he felt that he could stand
And brave all danger night and day
And bring his little band away

They sailed Nor need we paus to ask
If such a trust had been misplaced
For he was equal to the task
And evry turn of fortune faced
For six long years they stemed the tide
Through scenes of danger magnified
But oft a keg of gold had graced
The coffers whire they stored their gain
On that lone Island we have named

I need not tell how fortune flees
Returning then in time to save
The blood which softly called to shed
To free their passage on the wave
Nor need we tell how fickle fate
Stood ever ready at the gate
To open for the prudent brave
Who claimed that men could justly trade
In spite of laws unjustly made

To Boniam their old resort
Again they bounded o'er the sea
In form to make their years report
To gold bags which began to be
Quite bulkey. As each man could share
One hundred thousand waiting there
The time was come they all agree
To sell their ship and seek a home
And walk no more in paths unknown

Then to Shanghai they put away
With papers for the occasion
Resolveing there to make their stay
Brief as time could justly portion
When the old ship came into port
With yankee coulors past the fort
A lawful trader on the ocean
A cheer went up both fore and aft
As droped the anchor safe at last

The ship was sold and all did take
Passage in a homeward bounder
Nor was it long they had to wait
Befor the waters did surround them
Then homeward now through mist and storm
Right merely they dash along
With fortunes right. Or honest plunder
And as they roll. No smuglars fate
As vissions in the past dies [?] wake

And low again the mountains rise
Above the distant swelling main
Again the see as in the sky
Columbias hills peep forth again
The freshening gale drives on the shore
With all sail out they run before
And summer smiles along the train

MY THOUGHTS ON HOME DO DWELL

As triumph [?] from victors field
With fortunes self upon his shield

Charley stands at the cottage door
Whire he a child had found a home
A wanderer friendless sick and sore
In stranger land and yet alone
The Lady now he sees again
Though sorrow brings her not the same
Who with time their seeds hath sown
And on that brow once sweetly fair
We see the language of dispair

Now when Charley called her by name
She startled in a quick surprise
As though some news must give her pain
Or caus that lost hope to arrise
But when she knew her orphin boy
The wildness of a new found joy
Burst foarth in wonder. And replies
To questions followerd. Short in pace
Were answers on that wordy race

Here after waiting long long years
The wife now learns her husbands fate
And all those hopes those doubts and fears
Which time itself could not abate
Have opened here the mystic page
Whose silence through a dreary age
Of watching waiting long and late
Here learns at last the silent wave
Has rolled above his ocean grave

And whilst they yet were counting o'er
The many changes of the past
A footstep sounded at the door
And, e'er a question could be asked
A girlish form came [?] in

[53]

AND THE WHALE IS OURS

Gay as the voice of early spring
But when she saw the stranger guest
The rose and lilly seemed to meet
With pride and bluster on her cheek

Now let us jump a few short years
Whirein a quitness shall reign
And wearry days and doubtful tears
Seem half forgotten dreams of pain
When Charley learns how day by day
How their means has wasted away
He blesses his God for his own gain
And joyed that he could half repay
The kindness of that early day

So Charley bought the spreading fields
And cottage of his home before
And evry wish which pride conceals
His gold had brought around that door
The she who gave the stranger child
When winters blast blew drear and wild
A home. Though he was sick and sore
Shall now again in need receive
From the hand her bounties did relieve

A mansion fair in beauty raised
Whire spread the spacious meadows green
And natures smiles were its own praise
Or seemed half lonely for a queen
So Annie was the first to share
The bounties of a studied care
And one May morning there was seen
A gathering to that new abode
Of young and old in happy mood

Yes evry feature wore a smile
Therefore all was gay and joyful

MY THOUGHTS ON HOME DO DWELL

And merriment went round the while
Among the young and beautiful
Then Charley by the prettiest hand
Holds Annie who of cours must stand
Before the priest most dutiful
They remembered then who prophesied
That someday she should be his bride

Those golden hours must ever shine
On memory as bright and gay
Though life may darken these through time
Shall live to grace the endless day
And it will cheer the heart to bring
Those pleasures back on memories wing
The noontime of lifes summer day
Whire hope was crowned with all it asked
From the present future and the past

Now pretty names are fancies poses
Which bloom in innocence and pride
Friendship blooms in blushing roses
When love perchance may be allied
Now Sister Annie sounds most sweet
Since that presage is compleet
Which said that she could be his bride
He flies to her from doubt or fear
Whome those foreshadows must endear

And Charley now begins to live
Though oft before had blessed his lot
And deemed that he could never give
One thought to joyes which should not
Bring him near the wild wide sea
Where needs his soul must love to be
Such dreams are now it seems forgot
And in such changes he can bless
A joy which shall bring him rest

AND THE WHALE IS OURS

How blessed through a declineing life
The Lady dwelt in peaceful home
Beyond the dreams of want or strife
With Annie and her foster son
And thus among the friends she loved
Friends which a life of love had proved
And dreary years had cheered along
Her pitty for the orphen boy,
Are now re-paid in years of joy

Time which shall change each mans decree
Saw Charley prosper and one day
A little girl sat on his knee
He happy as a child at play
This girl grew up and pased from earth
Loved by all those who honor worth
In you my child revives one ray
Of that thy mother meekly mild
She was thy mother darling child

And I am Charley the little boy
Who wandered in the world alone
Whome selfish men would not employ
My tinny hands e'er they had grown
Yet still that Ladies gentle voice
Bade my young heart again rejoice
And told me I should have a home
God blessed her care in after years
And me to shield her age from fears

Yes Emma Dear those spreading trees
That shadow o'er yon mansion high
Are near the spot whire first I teased
To be employed. And she drew nigh
And bade me rest my little form
Within her cottage neat and warm

MY THOUGHTS ON HOME DO DWELL

And when my dampened cloths were dry
She told me that should be my home
To wander foarth no more alone

Here mem'ry paints youths glowing scenes
And here I learned to read and spell
Here in my wild romantic dreams
I did aspire as none shall tell
How o'er the ocean through the gale
I rode beneath the snowey sail
How oft my patience would rebel
When time rolled on with laging pace
And left me waiting for the race

And here I heard the welcome news
That I should cross the briney deep
Here fancy painted glowing views
Which I a wanderer was to meet
And mem'ry still points out the day
Whire in I proudly sailed away
A victory in itself most sweet
For evry hope my life could bring
Seamed nearing me on mystic wing

Oblivious self shall not efface
My boy love for the Rovers. Bride
As winged she onward in the race
Proudly o'er the gleaming tide
As if she heard the orders given
Yet though her mamoth sails were riven
Most willingly she would turn aside
And when the storm itself was past
I hailed her Monarch of the blast

And now my child tis growing late
It is not right that I have staid
Telling stories and made you wait

Here within this mighty shade
So let us leave this mirky air
And to our home again repair
Exposure oft before has made
The strongest form bow to decay
When health itself must pine away

Since you alone are left to me
A comfort in declineing years
If you were taken I should be
Left here alone to reap lifes fears
The friends which blessed my early pride
In youth in age through life allied
My all which love itself endears
Are gone when you I see no more
To leave me lonelier than of yore

Thus I the old mans story heard
Listning beyond the roadside wall
There he portrayed from word to word
Uncertain fortunes rise and fall
A Father hates his infant son
His Mother dead and he alone
Yet being friendless was not all
As when the strong themselves shall arm
And helpless infants seek to harm

Again we find the orphen boy
With friends far from his Fathers halls
Now he has changed his woes for joy
As captive freed from prison walls
Behold him bounding o'er the sea
As striveing for his distany
Then shipwreckd terrors on him falls
Again he leads a dareing band
Whire none shall gainsay his command

MY THOUGHTS ON HOME DO DWELL

Again we find him on the shore
Which gave him birth And in his turn
Can comfort her who long before
Had lent her care. that he might learn
How wisdoms ways could only bring.
Him blessings on times fleeting wing
And thus through life we trace him on
And he cries let come what will
Gods blessings makes me happy still

So then I said Gods wonderous ways
In secret works a right to man
And justice in each act displays
The power of his mighty hand
When the oppressor is oppressed
And on him turns the same distress
With witch he cursed his native land
For one hath said thy vengance stay
Leave that to him who will repay
End[12]

George Mills gave life on shore an even more melodramatic treatment in his episode from the Mexican War. This is one of the few works from the journals that abandons sea-life altogether: Mills chose a landlocked desert for his setting. 'Edwin Florance Or Circumstantial Evidence in the Camp of Gen. Taylor of the Mexican War' is unfinished, but its chapter and a half make entertaining reading.

The story begins when young Edwin, another half-orphan, leaves his mother and his betrothed to fight alongside General Taylor in Mexico. A Mexican bandit destroys the hero by making him appear to be a spy. Edwin's career is ruined, but he faces the firing squad bravely. Just before his death, he tries to clear himself. But there the manuscript breaks off. Presumably, Mills failed to think of a way to extricate his hero.

Despite several classic blunders – the bandit hisses 'ha ha' – 'Edwin Florance' might have been publishable. The hero, though naive, is of the genuine melodramatic type, and Vincent, the villain, is carefully developed.

The Mexican scene is given in some detail (although it is unlikely that cobras roam the desert). The story could certainly have reached the level of much of the storypaper and magazine fiction of the day without a great deal of rewriting. In the preface to another of his works, Mills claims to have written at least six novels, not including 'Edwin Florance.' He was certainly a facile writer of both fiction and verse.

Chapter 1
Go my boy and fight for Taylor and thy Countrys flag

'Tis hard to part with thee my Edwin. Oh my darling boy – remember thy Mothers counsel and never lay thy head down to rest without first asking the permission and blessing of God. Now Go. but Edwin my noble boy – remember your old and feeble Mother forget her not. for she will always raise a prayer to the God of Battles for the honor – virtue and prosperity of thee. thy mothers Pride Go Edwin thy poor old Mother's heart is well nigh bursting Go – and do thy duty and return with honor and virtue – here – to thy Mothers bossom, and God bless thee darling. Go – He's gone, my only child. – my darling Edwin – Oh Father of Heaven bless him – protect him in all his ways – He's gone the pride of my heart my only remaining child – Husband. – Children – all gone – and I am left to mourn and – and pray

Reader see you that Noble young Man Just quitting the roof of his Fathers before him – see you him – then then truly – tis a Noble look – His strong and sinewy limbs full of youth and vigor – full and compact chest. slim and withy form. straight and Gracefull figure. proudly erect. he leaves his dear old Mother – his only parent. leaves her for the honor of his country " and that Gentle Maiden Edwin – who no longer than the last evenings ramble confessed her love for thee. hast thou no Farewell Kiss for her who has promised to await thy Return with fond imptience to consumate a pure and holy plight of troth 'tween thou and Fair Jane Surely. his eyes turn that way as he passes a rural cottage half hidden by fine old Elms and wide spreading oaks. He hesitates – stops – looks up the Graveled walk with a sigh. he dashes a tear from his dark piercing eye and strides rapidly onward.

The sun is sending down its scorching rays, the dry and parched ground Lays cracked and baked hard the shrubs and wild flowing Grass in the plain beyond is withered and turned brown by the immensity of the beeting rays of the noonday Sun The air was still and sultry not a breath disturbed the withered foligge of the deep and inpenetrable Chapperal, or the lofty branches of the Beautifull cocanut tree that now and then could be seen raising its lofty head like unto some Lofty tower on a desert. alone in its Glory. everything was still as death around. at. length a long and Gradually rising whistle vibrated around. causing the lizzards and deadly Corbras to seek security in the murky ground of the Chapperal for scarcely had the sound died away before an other whistle. Long and loud proclaiming visitors around in the desolate regions of Sattillo Road. about ten miles from Walnut springs where the American Army then were camped.

Scarcely had the sounds died away e're a powerfully built Mexican emerged from an ajoining thicket. and sautering carelessly towards whence the answering whistle was heard

He wore a large wide Brimed Sombrero *set carelessly on one side of his head. his features were coarse and irregular – yet a small black eagle eye showed a quickness of apprehension and subtility of thought unworthy of the impression first formed*

He was heavily armed. although no one could see anything but a heavy rifle which he weilded with the ease and dexterity of one long used to the handling of such

His dress consisted of a light tricollored poncho. *which concealed a brace of duelling pistols of Mantons Make – a glistning dagger thrust into his bossom. concealed all by his countrys apology for a coat – the poncho.*

He sauntered carelessly up the Noted Road ever and anon casting quick and furtive glances around. reaching at length the cover of a thicket of considerable extent he awaited the approach of a young Man dressed as a seargent of the American Army – surely that tall and Manly form we have seen somewhere before those well formed limbs – dark and flashing eye a complexion slightly turned by exposure to the sun. surely it must be – Florance. who left his Mother. his home. and his hearts first love not quite a year ago. and now see him. oh what would that fond Mother say could she see her darling boy as he steped forth in all the concious pride of honor deserved and integrity of Purpose. But what does he with Vincent. the Spy. his appointed meeting alone – ten miles beyond the limits of the Camp. tis strange. tis pasing strange. yet their conversation will show.

Well Senor. Mexican what would you with me. I have come at your bidding. not through servitude but to show thee. I bear no ill will towards you and still fear you not. our slight quarrel was brought on by yourself and consequently you received your reward. but explain those few misterious words you used in your letter.

Not so fast Serargent Florance. you know I am hasty of temper and cannot bear contradiction and our slight Misunderstanding orrinated from that defect in my temper. but I will show you that I also bear no ill will towards thee by putting you in a way to render Taylor a service and the reward shall be your promotion it is a light service on your part and will benefit your Country Greatly

But why did you not seek out some other source for delivering these news. than by making me the agent. I begin to mistrust your intentions

No no Seargent Florance. I could not get the Papers carried by so trustworthy as yourself and you know I am denied the camp. and wishing to prove to General Taylor that he reposes confidence in wrong persons. and to Clear myself from suspision. I chose you because I know you can be relied on and twill be doing you a service which will requite the wrong I once done you. you are in favor with your Comanding officers. and your assertion will be relied upon more than any other one I know of. now you see why I choose you and it lays with you altogather if you will convey these papers or No. you have your choice –

Well Viencent you speak candidly and like a person wishing to do justice. yet I do not like your features or their expression whilst you have been talking with me. you see I am on the lookout. nevertheless I will take these papers as you said provided there is no conditions affixed more than in the delivery of them

You do me wrong Seargent Florance to doubt. you will see the time when your predjudice will be removed and to thank me in the Bargain but here are the papers. and do not deliver them till tomorrow at 9 A.M. there will be a certain individual arrive at camp. then deliver them any time after his arrival Keep them close for they are of importance. I've got to go some ten miles to the wrieght of superceedence on an estate from here. North East. so I will not keep you waiting. So Good Bye. Addois

Well Good Day Vincent. Addois. said Florance, and taking a quick step was soon out of sight of Vincent. whose face lit up with a simile of triumph and of vengeance gained as he said through his clenched teeth Go. Boy – you will soon learn the reward of Vincents hate and cause to thank him – ha – ha – ha –

MY THOUGHTS ON HOME DO DWELL

Edwin Florance Or Circumstantial Evidence
Chapter Seccond

With pride and honor's Concious step
He Marched to meet his death
1.5.13 . . .

"*How is this. Major Bliss. do we harbour traitors then by Heavens they shall have the reward due them. this is news indeed and such as will admit of no delay. make out a warrant for the arrest of. let me see. whats the name. pass that letter to me again. oh. here 'tis Make out an orde for the immediate arrest of Seargent Florance of the 2nd Light Infantry. then send the orderly Seargent. with his gaurd to search his Effects. and. meanwhile send the person here who brought this letter from the spy*

He's gone. went immediately after delivering the letter General. but I will send out after him if you wish. he cannot be far off. and quickly overtaken. answered Major Bliss who was buisy. making out the warrent.

No. never mind he could be of little service to the case. what was he a camp lounger or one of the Citizens hereabouts.

I know not General. he was never seen in camp before. where shall his quarters be General in the old Guard or in the guard house.

Yes. sir. put him in double shackles with a sentry. in the old Guard. and have his papers all. Enlistment. bills. all brought hither. at the court. will sit on Court Martial. at ten. have him brought. at the opening.

Yes. General. the warrant is full sir and shall be sent directly. Gaurd; Wheres Ho. without. Seargent. of the Gaurd. Advance. and receive dispatches. here. take this warant and see it executed with out delay confine him in the Gaurd with constant Sentries and let him escape at their perril. He saw twas useless to try and evade the direct and undisputed proof of his guilt. twas hard to know that he was innocent yet must die. far from home and dear loved friends. no kind and sympathising Friend to soothe the last of him who was to die the death of a traitor.

Vincent bore no innocent part in the condemntion of Edwin and he showed his mallice in so forward a maner that many of Edwins Friends or Comrades had a suspicion of treatchery. and they cast angry Glances to wards the spy. yet he seemed not to notice them. that same cold calm and steady inpenetrable look. seemed to defy their abillity to fathome the deep laid plot of the wily spy His trial was not of long duration such positive proof had been given that his fate was sealed and Sentence passed in an inconceivable short space of time. Edwin turned pale as he heard a low chuckle at his Elbow and turning round he saw Vincent at his side almost. and bending ever towards Edwin hissed between his clenched teeth

"dost thou remember when you struck me some days ago. you do I warrant. that time proud American. dog of white race. you made Vincent an Enemy to you. and now you have thy reward and I revenge. ha. ha. sweet Revenge.

"You triumph now. but know you swarthy son of a perfideous race. that I fear you not I scorn you as I would a dog. – go – and take an inocent mans curse. with you. a low and hissing. ha – ha – ha – was all he heard or see of Viencent in the hurry of the patrol Gaurd.

The Crier of the court Colenl Yates. steped up to the prisinor and wished to know if he had any thing to say or any request to make.

answered. I should like to say a few words to those present. and sir if you will be so kind as to send this letter and locket to its address you will confer an oblegation which I can never repay. Seargent Florance. I have allways thought a great deal of you and beleive me. I will see that these are sent with due dispatch and – but he was inturupted by Taylor who rose and eyeing the Prisinor Sharply for a few moments said Has the Prisinor anything to say before proceeding to Execution. if so the Court has granted liberty. What ho there Gaurds remove the prisinors Irons. and stay as Sentry. after this being done. Florance arose slowly and as his tall manly form stood upright and proudly Erect. he said in a voice clear and Firm

"Commander in Chief – and Aids to the Staff – and Comrades all. I stand before you a condemned Traitor. but what I am about to say I pray you to consider it as though twas but yesterday when In all the pride of Manhoods Noblest virtue on my brow. and the Friendship of Many of the Glorious men that now compose the American Army. infusing confidence and respect – consider as though I said it then and then call Edwin Florance a Traitor to His Country. to every Manly feeling and every virtue lost. if ye can. is it possible most Noble Generals that you will take a [?] spys statements. before you will an American Soldiers. who, before this villians double damned villiany had placed me in this precarious situation was held to be worthy of the confidence of his comander. and of comarades, all. and what I am now about to say is

the simple [Varity?] of parts which I am unable to prove. but which I hope the court will give me credit for the truth. twenty two hours after the Mexican spy was prohibited visiting the camp and just two hours before the Countersign was void a mesage came to me inviting me to come at a place affixed for the purpose of giving[13]

Hiram King's doubts about the wisdom of thinking too often or too directly about home were probably shared by many whalemen. The few writings that depart from such clichés as 'there's no place like home' were, like Goram's 'We ll soon be there,' written close to the time of return, when the pain of departure had been replaced by the pleasure of anticipation. And, while a few whalemen's journals do contain comments about loved ones on shore, the home ties that bound men who could plan a three-year absence were probably loose ones to begin with.

CHAPTER THREE

AN ETERNITY OF LOVE

LIKE dreams of home, thoughts of love inspired whalemen to creative writing. However, aside from the relatively rare wife who accompanied her captain husband, they had few direct models. The women they met were usually natives. And, while such encounters were often related with obvious pleasure as part of a day's entry, they were seldom memorialized in either prose or verse. Even local color was generally ignored. William Macy's and William Wilson's poems about south sea island women and Ambrose Bates's novella of an Eskimo femme fatale are remarkable exceptions.

In general, and perhaps as a result of distance both in space and time, the whalemen's love poetry was reserved for more conventional romantic subjects: sweethearts and wives at home.

Many writers adapted popular songs and poetry to their own needs. In the early 1840's, William Weeden of Rhode Island was seriously troubled during most of his voyage on the *John & Edward*. There was a mutiny on board, and Weeden was disturbed as well by recurring dreams of the death of Ellen, 'my love, my life, my wife.' Many of the approximately fifteen poems in Weeden's journal were copied from such authors as Milton and Goldsmith, and most were probably taken from newspapers. The sentiments are typical of his time, celebrating the spiritual joys of marriage. Weeden made use of such work by inserting Ellen's name at crucial points in others' poems. His spelling of 'weeded Love' is especially endearing.

> *with Thee My E ... I will brave all human hate*
> *Nor fear the ills of cruel fate*
> *In vain shall foes attempt to move*
> *My guiding star is __ __ weeded Love*

[67]

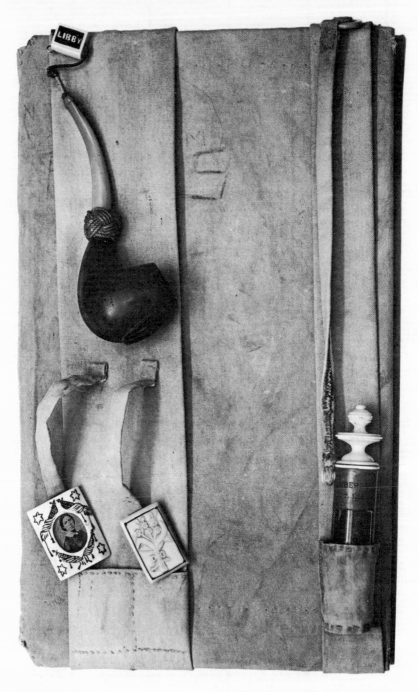

During the American Civil War, while serving with the Eighteenth
Massachusetts Volunteers, Frederick Smith carried a tiny likeness of a
sweetheart or wife. In her hand-carved bone frame, she later adorned the
sailcloth cover of Smith's 1865–1866 *Herald* journal.

AN ETERNITY OF LOVE

How can I then desponding be
while I – My E – am blest with Thee

Yes the bright Star of : : weded Love
Shall banish evry care
For cheered by thee, My life – My Dove
My heart will neer despair
And when beyond this world we have paſsed
Oh – shall our tender love still last
Yes – an Eternity of love
Shall flow in purer streams above
For Heaven would not be Heaven to me
Were I unblest My Ellen with Thee[1]

A later captain, Frederick H. Smith of Fairhaven, also wrote poems filled with generalized sentiments about his wife and love. The same journal has a magnificent illustration, done in watercolor with an attention to detail that is missing in the poems, of a voluptuous dancing girl performing in a saloon.

One of Smith's poems is an acrostic on his wife's name. This was a relatively common form for whalemen journalists, although usually done on the name of the ship.

Acrostic

S – allie my dear, its Sunday morn,
a – nd I am far away from Home.
l – ong seems the time that I've been gone,
l – onger the time that I must roam.
i – hope that I the time may see,
e – ver to stay at Home with thee.

G – one is the Sun ended the day

S – hadows of night around us fall
m – aking one sunday less to stay
i – nside of Petrels wooden wall.
t – hat you tonight Dear one may have
h – appiness and health is all I crave.[2]

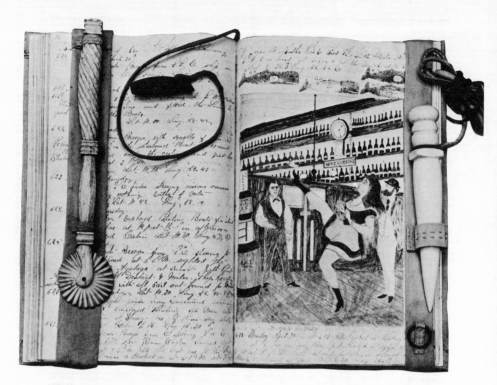

While skipper of the *Petrel*, 1871–1874, Captain Frederick Smith composed poetry to his wife Sallie in his journal. He also busied himself with scrimshaw and thoughts of other things. Smith's bookmark served as a whale tally stamp.

Smith had indeed stayed long at sea; he had been away two years when he wrote his 'Acrostic.' A second poem, 'Home again with Sallie,' is obviously a case of wishful thinking – as is, perhaps, the dancing girl and the saloon.

Home again with Sallie

Home again! spared the perils of years,
Spared of rough seas and rougher lands,
And I look in your eyes once, once again,
Hear your voice and grasp your hands;

Not changed the least, least bit in the world;
Not changed a day as it seems to me!
The same dear face, the same old home –
All the same as it used to be.[3]

AN ETERNITY OF LOVE

Ambrose Bates composed a sad love poem which rejects such tactics as Hiram King's refusal to think of home for fear of being driven mad. Bates prizes his memories primarily because they include his Annie – whose name he gives to the heroine of 'The Grandfathers Story,' even though many of his thoughts of the past are painful.

Cumberland Inlet April 1866

There is a joy I love. Though now
It dwells on mem'ries waste
Which dimly here. yet sparkles from
The haunts of early days

Could I but pass from mortal care
Which is but doubt and pain
And from a world of misory turn
To dust from whence I came

And there forget those weary years
My Annie with the rest
I should shrink from such a change
And choose to live unblest.

Then loose that joy which o'er my soul
In vissions of the past
Calls up that mountain bliss of mine
Which could not did not last

Were I to sleep a thousand years
Without one little dream
Then consiousness return again
In that bewildered scene

The newest thought which bade me wake
As midnight lightnings flash
Would bring to me on memries wing
Those moments of the past

And in that instant hopes of years
Would gather bright as new

And then again to leave me still
With happiness in view

But I shall prise each instinct which
Reminds me of that joy
More then will match a thousand years
Though poisoned with alloy

Then let me live for what is past
Though nothing more can claim
For memory is my only hope
The future but a name[4]

The parting of lovers was a common subject in whalemen's love poetry. An early example is William Silver's strangely impersonal farewell poem to his 'love.' At first Silver seems to have an actual sweetheart in mind, but as the poem proceeds it becomes apparent that Silver's regret at leaving home is his true subject.

Ship Bengal at Sea Feb 1835

Oh say shall the morns early gale
waft me from the arms of my love home
or say am I yet to bewail
misfortune has caused me to roame
Oh say must I end these fond hours
does misfortune her quest oer flow
Oh drownd me in sympathic showers
Yes love I must bid you adieu

With care have I tasted life charms
on the bosom of friendship and love
but now I am forced from thine arms
the wide billowing ocean to roam
the sun spreads his lucid lucid aray
while the tune that is sung yo heave ho
our anchor is hove short and away
I come love to bid you adieu

> *The day dawns in the east*
> *the Landsafse [?] or twilight I view*
> *the breeze gently blows from the West*
> *it blows love to bear me from you*
>
> *When by tempests I am tost to and fro*
> *or in storms I am lifted from you*
> *one thought on your breast may it dwell*
> *for the one that now bids you adieu*
>
> *Adieu to columbias proud fields*
> *adieu to the daughters she bore*
> *and adieu to the sun that now gealds*
> *and adieu to humanityes shore*
>
> *Our canvess is spread to the breese*
> *our signals are wavering in wind*
> *Love I am hurried away to the seas*
> *an emblem of love fare you well*[5]

Silver's 'love' may have been purely imaginary. Joseph E. Ray, a Nantucket boatsteerer and a talented illustrator, wrote a farewell poem addressed to an actual woman. Ray's conventional poem illustrates what must have been an uncommon situation for a working whaleman on his travels: a meeting and friendship with a genteel young lady, all the more unusual for taking place on a tiny island in the South Pacific. Indeed, the lines suggest Ray may have felt a great deal more than friendship for his 'sweet friend' Anna.

> *Lines Respectfully inscribed to Miss Anna McCoy*
> *at Norfolk Island, Dec. 3rd 1857*
>
> *Dearest Anna. now fare well*
> *Since fate Compells us thus to part*
> *May God protect thee from life's ills*
> *And guard the tablets of thine heart.*
> *May guardian Angels. hover O'er thee*
> *In thy hour of trial. sweet friend.*

And bear thee o'er life's dreary path
E'en to thy earthly journeys end.

It is the earnest prayer of one
Whose bound to thee by friendship's sacred ties
To see thee joined in hymen's holy bonds
With the dearest object of thy choice
May God protect him as well as thee
And join thy hearts with holy love
Ensure thee Happiness and peace
And countless blessings from above

But. Anna! in thy memory yet
Cherish one thought of the absent sailor boy
Forget him not. when far away
Where his sorrows'll turn to joy
Oh! Pray God to guide his gallant Bark
Safe O'er the troubled Sea
To his own dear native land so fair
In the regions of the free.[6]

William H. Macy of Nantucket wrote a quite different farewell poem commemorating a more likely love affair than Ray's. Macy's picture of his 'Island maid' is a romantic one, but laced with comedy as the subtitle warns.

My Island Maid

Love founded on ten minutes acquaintance in the bush

Who is't that thou seekest in yon wood so green
Where so seldom is aught but the birds to be seen
Who is't that thou seekest in yonder deep shade
Tis my hearts' dearest treasure my fair Island maid

And whose is that form that now flits through the trees
With motion unequalled for beauty and ease

Now lovely as Venus now shrouded in shade
She waits for my coming – my fair Island maid

Tis a dream! Tis a vision! tis nought of this earth
Tis something to which my wild fancy gives birth
Tis the fancy of tender affections betrayed
As I gaze on the form of my fair Island maid

Her hair in long ringlets her face half conceals
While her bosom betrays the deep love that she feels
As together we linger in yonder cool shade
And enraptured I gaze on my fair Island maid

No necklace of rubies encircles her neck
Nor in jewels nor gold, nor in satin's she's decked
But sooner with her would I roam in the shade
Than with many more gay than my fair Island maid

Soon Soon must I leave her in sorrow to mourn
Far o'er the wide sea perhaps ne'er to return
But though seas roll between us ne'er shall memory fade
But I'll cease not to think of my fair Island maid

Her image o'er the ocean my beacon shall be
And conduct me in safety far o'er the deep sea
And may I soon return to that cool pleasant shade
And my hearts only treasure my fair Island maid[7]

William H. Wilson's 'Queen of Otaheite' gives a less respectful report of a 'fair Island maid.' As well as being a rare depiction of a native girl, Wilson's poem is one of the few examples of nonsense verse to be found in the journals. The refrain, made up of nonsense syllables, is reminiscent of 'O Huncamunca, Huncamunca O,' from Fielding's burlesque play, *The Tragedy of Tragedies.* The names 'Humphrey' and 'Crow' may be borrowed from Smollett, a novelist read by many whalemen. Much of the rest of the song is somewhat puzzling. Does being 'reversed . . . from head to foot' simply mean being turned upside down? Or is this period pornography? In fact, what does happen at the end? Cannibalism, surely, but . . . .

Queen of Otaheite

In Otaheite, I have heard say
a huge fat maid walked out,
Her head was like a mourning coach
it was so long and black O,
Her eyes were like two cocoa nuts;
and a braſs ring through her snout
And they called her Unca, Punca, Wunca, Hoca, Coley, Bargo, O,
As she waddled through the woods one day, Palthy, Palthing, lost her way,
the sun was in a burning ray, she squatted under a high tree, And with fatigue
began to pant sat herself down upon a plant, Just like a female elephant was the
queen of Otaheite,
As Punca, Wunca, lay asleep, two monkeys from a tree
Come down and rooled off the bank into the inner slop O,
She floated down the stream for miles, I think 'twas thirty-three,
And like some Humphry, I heard sink to take a watery nap O,
The water bubbled high and one Chief Crow came rowing by,
In his canoe, and heard the cry, and stopped just as he might see
What it was moving in the deep, nimble dived down to take a peep
And for some hours he fell asleep, with the queen of Otaheite.

Now just before the sun went down, Chief Crow quick arose
And took her home to his own hut, while she was in a dose
Upon his mat he took his seat, and reversed her there from head to foot,
Of human flesh he made her eat; I'll sleep with you to night, O!
And they gorged away on flesh and figs, and played a few such seeming rigs
Both went to sleep, and snored like pigs – did the Queen of Otaheite
Now he one day contrived a plan to take her to her home,
For she had stormed the hut of all eatables and stock O,
So he popped her into his canoe, and towed her off to Kinknmru,
For if her blood was in a Q, or the blue devils smight, O!
And the Queen's ribs began to punch, and doubled old Crow in a bunch
And cut them up for her own lunch, a monstrous trick in Otaheite,

Chorus: Tong-a-song-a-ching-a-song-pick-a nick-a-ho-ta-ra-ho-ca-punca,
    munca, chunco——!⁸

AN ETERNITY OF LOVE

George Howland, one of the last of the creative writers on board whale-ships, was the coauthor of the only openly pornographic, or even bawdy, work uncovered in all the journals. In fact, extremely few pornographic written items, copied or original, are in the major public whaling collections: two versions, in varying conditions of completion, of 'Frozen Limb,' the original work reprinted below; two copies of a supposed letter from a bride to a friend, describing her wedding night; a loose verse description of two people in bed whose bodies are portrayed in terms of different animals and poultry; and two copies of a poem about a lady passenger's dress being blown over her head. In addition, William Wilson's 'Queen of Otaheite' (above) probably qualifies.

It is, at first, surprising that pornography, either original or copied, fills so little space in the whalemen's journals. But the journalists were more often educated members of the cabin or the steerage than the forecastle, and as such may have learned the restraint proper in Victorian times. Although none of these journals was intended for immediate publication, many journalists expected family or friends to read their work and may have consciously avoided controversial topics and language.[9] Then too, since many journals have not survived or have had pages removed, it is likely that potentially embarrassing work was simply destroyed by the journalist himself, his wife, a descendant, or a well-meaning manuscript custodian in a local historical society.

Howland and Russell collaborated on 'Frozen Limb' toward the end of their voyage on the *Pioneer* in the mid-1870's. Both authors were from Dartmouth, Massachusetts,[10] and probably knew each other before sailing, although Russell, second mate on the *Pioneer*, was nine years older than Howland. Russell, who kept the detailed reading list of sensational fiction described in chapter I, was apparently the lesser contributor. His journal's version is incomplete. George Howland's contains the finished poem.

Frozen Limb

one cold frosty eaving
as her Farther lay Sleeping
I taped at the window
where Mary did lay

by the light of the taper
I saw her come creeping
and whose at my window
she Softly did say

it is I my Dear mary
Benighted and weary
My Limbs are all Frozen
I am wet to the Skin
I prey you take pitty
And kindly admit me
At last She concented
I climbed and got in

She scarce had perceived me
Before I enroled her
Hugging and kissing
her every charm
She says you deceived me
You have falsly told me
That your limbs were all fozzen
But I find them quite warm

Oh Mary dear mary
This bossom I am presing
Porseses more beauty
More whiteness then snow
And the little white hand
I am so tenderly squeezing
Might well freeze the limb
that we melted Just now

She eagerly grasped it
And tenderly clasped it
Crying Leubin dear Leubin
The truth is quite plain
For the more I am Squeezing
The harder Its freezing

AN ETERNITY OF LOVE

And now Its quite stiff
Let us melt it again

O Leubin dear Leubin
Its now you must leave me
Head not the cold the hail or the rain
But if the freezing
Your limbs should
Keep teasing
Come back to me quickly
And we will melt them again
End[11]

Not all writers confined themselves to sorrowful farewell poems or playful burlesques when they wrote of women and love. Samuel T. Braley, whose tributes to his home and wife appear in chapter II, is one of the most introspective of the whalemen writers. His thoughts about women in general, and his wife in particular, appear frequently in his journals and reveal an unusual level of expressed emotion.

In an early journal, written in his late twenties when he was newly married, Captain Braley betrays some hostility towards the opposite sex. An entry in the back pages of this *Arab* journal (1845–1849) combines bitter remarks on the physical hardships of whaling life with even more bitter thoughts of the 'trap' of love.

July the 14th 1848

This day is the fourteenth aneversera of my Sailors life. In the time I have pased from youth to manhood; an although not thirty years of age, I find myself alredy in the decline of life. When I look back on my past life how plain I can see the truth of the saying of the Wise man; that all things under the Sun are but vanity and vexation of Spirrit

When I started on my first voyage I formed withen my self the resolution to be one day master of a Ship and in that capasity aquire welth suffitient to support me in the decline of life; I was well aware that I must sacrifise all my best days in order to obtain it but I paid but little head to that and presed forward through whatever obsticals presented thenselves, and applied myself so closely to my profession that I have broke my constitution, and have now before me all the horrows of a miserable life; but I gained the point at which I amed, in the first respect, and am now nearly redy to return home after 3 years toil with any thing but a good voyage; which, of course disappoints me in the second; but I will not antisipate.

But why did I wish for welth twas that bane of man Woman; and knowing from my own feelings that I should be unhappy in any circumstances without a dose of mans bane; evry oppertunity that I had I employed myself in looking for one with whome I mite unite myself and be happy; but I saught in vain, and had given up the idea when I caught sight of a remarkably bright eye set in a very intelectual face, and I e're I was aware of it, was Caught like all other fools but I bless the trap that caught me and would not like to be free [12]

Another passage is even more resentful:

What is the cause of a man's going to sea; Answer, Woman. What is the affect; Answer. Grey hares, or none at all a black face full of rinkles, for which women dispise him. And after having thrown the vigor of youth and manhood to the winds he findes himself an old man at 35 when his pockets are em'ty

A plge on this salt water; it wear a man down worse than six wives would if they all had red hair. I never will alow any of my boys to go to SALT. sea, no any of my deaighter to marry Sailors unles hes a Captain in which case mum. [13]

Although Braley's reports of his deteriorating health may have been true for many other whalemen, his comments are a bit misleading. A hypochondriac, not yet thirty, Braley filled his journals with detailed descriptions of his ill health. He barely recovers from one disorder before another takes its place. While illness at sea was a serious business, Braley luxuriates in many nearly obsessive accountings.

But the two selections are not characteristic of Braley's feelings toward his wife. Many more passages are just as passionate in his love for her, for Braley was a man capable of expressing all his emotions. It is one of his chief attractions that he does so. The examples above can safely be attributed to periods of despondency to which most whalemen, indeed most people, are susceptible.

On the pages immediately following the above selections, Braley reasserts his more constant emotion in a love poem. These affectionate verses are full of concern for his young wife, Mary Ann, whose trials he describes in metaphors of the sea. Only a minor note of reproach remains, and Braley ends lovingly.

His reference in stanza seven to his hurried departure is not exaggerated. He had returned on the *Arab* on 2 October 1845, and left again on November 22nd of the same year. Like most whaling captains' wives, Mary Ann seldom saw her husband.

Musings; ten days from home; after a storm

The night geathers darkly, the heavens are scowling
With terror the elements seam to be charged;
The lightnings bright flash, and horse thunder's long growl
Asks in plain accents are you prepaired

For the coming tempest that now hovers ore you
Thretning to engulf you in Ocean's dark wave
To rend from the timbers the plank that's beneath you
And leave you to perish with no arm to save

Yes, tempests may howl round, and seas yan to engulf us
And in many shapes may appear deaths grim form;
We will trust in Him who once stilled the tempest
And rules now, as then, the storm and the calm.

Then let us be cheared with bright hopes of the future
Nor render our soules to the fiend of despair
Knowing that in Him we all have a saviour
Whose love is far better than a brothers fond care.

O had I the hope that the Christian posseseth
That anchor to the soule both stedfast and shure
Then well mite smile at the care that oppeseth
And feal in the tempest and calm quite secure

Then Mary be chearful, nor mourn at my absence
Though Ocean divides I'm still ever thine
Still hope to be cheared by the smile of thy presence
And chear thy lone heart with the sunshine of mine

I know it was needfull for us to be parted
But it seamed rather hard to be parted so soon
Sent to be with thee lond enough to find thee true hearted
Then hurried away to be absent so long

Indeed it was hard to leave you dear Mary
And roam far away over Ocean's dark wave
But a thousand times harder t'would be to be with you
And see you in wand when I could not save.

For thee, and thee only I'm willing to suffer,
All the privations that fall to my lot
And feal proud in rouming over the blue water
Hoping that by thee I am never forgot.

Thou knowest that I love thee, not for thy beauty
Although thou arte lovely as lovely can be
T'is not out of pitty – nor yet out of duty
But like the Gentiles of old, because you love me

I rest on the caution that you gave wen left you
And it chears my lone heart in many a dark hour
T'was not to forget there was one that still loves you
Let foes do the worst that lay in their power

O when I look forward on the voyage thats before me
On the months that must pass o're wee meet again
My Sperrit grows Sick, my heart dies within me
To think that perhaps we may not meet again

If thus its decreed by our allwise Creator
That we meet no more in this vale of tears
May I be prepaired to join you with that number
Where the presence of the Lamb shall calm evry fear.

AN ETERNITY OF LOVE

Finely dear Mary to Him I commend you
Whose grace is suffitiant in each trying hour
May He ever be redy to guide and defend
And not let affliction thy soul overpower.[14]

The same section of this journal contains an even more touching narration about 'her that is as dear to me as life.' Braley's marginal note, halfway through, asks 'dont laff at the simille [simile] for it is true.' It would take a hard-hearted reader to scorn the retelling of this dream.

What pleasure is there in this cold world that can eaqual the return to a young, pritty Wife after an absence of three long years: I have tried, I beleave about all kinds in the course of my life, which now may be reconed at thirty years, but never in all that I have antisipated and much less in all that I have enjoyed, have I ever felt so supreemely happy as I did about twelve hours ago, when driving up in bugy like Jehu I run close along side of the board fence that is in front of sertain house, and without stoping to hitch the horse, I clear the carriage and fence at one leap, take a few strides, I am at the doar, I opene it and the next to the left hand, and I see coming from the opposite side of the room – (as none but a woman that loves you can) her that is as dear to me as life as quick as thought she is in my armes; I hold the dear realily; I feal her soft armes round my neck; I feal her warm breath upon my cheek; our lips meet and mingle in one long heart-melting kiss, and cling to each other as though they could not sever. . . . "Capt Braley! the Ship wont bear the Main-sail any longer," – what a transition! quick as thought I an transported from Rochester Mass. to the Gulph Manar; my horse and carriage is turned into a Ship, her cabbin is my Wife's sitting room; and my Wife, Alas! that it should be so, is turned into a pillow; (not salt) but the embrace was as real, at least on my part for I do not think that my Wife would wish to be pressed any closer to my boosom than the pillow was, nor be spurned away with any more contempt; as for the Ship carring, or draging the Mainsail, it was much the same to me for a few minets Oh the dred reality; a gail of wind lee shore and no whales HOPE[15]

Braley's next journal, kept on the *Arab* in 1849–1852 when he was in his early thirties, starts off with a decorative title page which reads: 'Journal of a Whaling voyage, With reflections & musings By Samuel T. Braley. To Mrs. Samuel T. Braley This volume is inscribed With evry fealing of Love and esteem By her Loving Husband.'[16]

His stay between voyages had been only a little longer this time: 2 June to 21 November 1849. But the journal seems designed to make Mary Ann's waiting easier, at least on the next trip. Each entry begins with a brief description of the day's activities in terse logbook style; the rest of each large page is filled with reminiscence and verse. Each entry closes with a variation on 'good night, my dove, my love, my wife.'

Several of Braley's efforts are quite serious, if conventional, love poems, frequently embedded among matter-of-fact or even comic anecdotes and observations. Once, in a characteristically cheerful mood, Sam 'wound up his poetry machine' to write about his picture of Mary Ann. The result is an affectionate poem, surrounded with lighthearted remarks in prose. The references to fortune, 'like all the females; fickle as the wind,' are clearly meant in jest. And, unconventionally, Sam emends his remembered days past to remembered nights.

I am in East Longitude again, where I mist remain 2, 3, or 4 years; just as fortune pleases who is like all the females; fickle as the wind but always likes to bestow her favours on the young; but I hope I am not so old yet but what I shall get a smile or two more from the Coquet. I have been writing some lines on your likeness – don't laff for my machine is out of order and it wont grind good no how

> *Dear little token of my absent love,*
> *How much my eyes delight to gase on thee;*
> *T'was given to me; in forreigh clime to prove*
> *How well the giver still remembered me.*

> *And as I gaze into thy love-lit eye,*
> *Beaming with fondness for the cherished one*
> *I rings from out my heart the bitter sigh,*
> *For thou arte far away, and I am all alone*

> *I gaze, and gaze, till the fond tear drop starts*
> *O'er joys departed: – of all but hope bereft*

AN ETERNITY OF LOVE

Thine image still is in my heart of hearts
There to remain untill erased by death.

Sometimes in thought I am transported back
To sceans in days (or rather nights) that are past.
In rapture I seek to press thy glowing lips, Alas!
The spell is broke; I, is nothing but cold glass.

I have been reading the pictorial discription of the United States and I like
it much; we have a fine fair wind and our old ship is bounding away like a
pig through the mire my semille is rather vulger, but trew to the life Good
night Lady, Love, Darling, Dove [17]

In a later journal for the same voyage, Braley entered a love poem taking
Mary Ann's point of view. The reference to 'pratling little "Henry"' in
the third stanza shows Braley's distinctive personalizing touch.

Sail making and thinking of thee and home and what you have written in your
letters about my being so long away and only see what pretty lines can be mad
out of it for I suppose you think sometimes thus

Linger not long – Home is not home without thee
Its dearest tokens only make me mourn
Oh! let its memory, like a chain about thee
Gently compel, and hasten thy return

Linger not long – Though welth should woo thy staying
Bethink thee can the hope of gain though dear
Compinsate for the grief of thy long delaying
Costs the poor heart that sighs to have thee heer

Linger not long – how shall I watch thy coming
As evenings shaddows stretch o'er moor an fell
When the wild Sea hath sceased her weary humming
And silence hangs on all things like a spell

How shall I watch for thee when feares grow stronger
As night grows dark and darker on the hill

And then I sigh when I can watch no longer
Oh thou art absent Thou art absent still

Yet should I grieve not though the eye that seeth me
Gazeth through tears that make its splendour dull
For oh! I sometimes fear when thou art with me
My cup of happiness is all too full

Haste, hast thee home unto thy lowly dwelling
Hast as a bird unto its peacefull nest
Haste as a skiff when tempests wild are swelling
Flies to its haven of secured rest.

Not linger there far from thy loved one straying,
In hopes of wining in a bootles chase
No broken voyage is e're patched up by staying:
Haste, haste my wanderer to my fond embrace.

Linger not long – Think how sad and lonely
The hours have drged till three long years have gon
With naught to cheer but pratling little 'Henry'
His voice sounds like thee, yet tis not thine own

Linger not long – But haste to cheer thy Mary
E'er hope's bright star enshrouded fades from sight
I'm sick at heart; I'm sad, and lone, and wearry,
Why stay so long? Am I forgotten quite?

No dearest you are not forgotten and I am coming
home one of these days I hope within this year yet.[18]

Braley's hope to return within the year was fulfilled. But his voyages as a whaling captain continued, with only short breaks, until 1857, then resumed in the mid-1860's into the early 1870's.[19] The Kendall Whaling Museum's seven Braley journals reveal a decline in literary quality over the years. The journals of his late twenties and early thirties, however, are among the most thoughtful and inventive in any collection. Mary Ann surely must have enjoyed reading them.

AN ETERNITY OF LOVE

George Mills, author of 'Edwin Florance,' also turned his narrative energies to the subject of love. In what he claims is his sixth novel, Mills describes the course of an imagined courtship between a close friend of his, the second mate, and a girl on shore. 'Frank Leman, Or: A Month. in the Country' is a model story in many ways. Judging by the four other titles Mills lists, as well as his unfinished melodrama already discussed, a simple narration of successful love and courtship was an unusual venture for Mills, as it was for most contemporary writers.

In another place in this same journal, which contains entries for three different voyages, Mills identifies his friend John Martin as the hero of 'Frank Leman.'

Miscellaneous Characters

3rd Good looks. and rich cloths always commands respect. Therefore to Keep the Maxim alive we take Mr John. Martin. Seccond Mate, for our next character. which is his due. Stands five feet seven and a half. on a sheet of paper. dark auburn hair. dark blue eyes. A nose betwixt Acqueline and Roman. thin lips. dark red whiskers. prominent chin. Thin face. and florid Complection light form full of pith and Blue veins. Uses proper language upon all occasions. fond of Litteary and Historical works. reads a Novel now and then. verry fond of jokes and comic songs seldom smiles but when he is pleased. Never protracts a dispute when he knows he is wrong. Finds fault when there's a reason Admires dress in himself also in others knows a pretty girl when he sees her. Never shows fight but in anger. can laugh when occasion calls for it. verry perticular in his toilette. admires the same in others. Generous and Kind to those who uses him according to gunter. Verry fond of Pets. more particular of Beauty. Allias Lemans. admires practical seamanship. understands it with ability drinks verry little consequently seldom if ever gets Gentlemanly Excited. Verry particular in his diet. seldom eats anything he dont like without he's hungray. Understands himself correctly. and conducts himself with proptitity to the best of his Knowledge seldom goes to extreams without it is walking the decks of a coald Night verry Fast after a fish. No doubt is entertained concerning his Moralts. is verry fond of good living drinks swanky tu Kill don't he. who prepares it[20]

[87]

The opening remarks to the story suggest that Mills's friendship with Martin-'Leman' continued. What probably occurred, then, was not unusual for whalemen: the two met, became friends, and transferred together from one whaleship to another in the Pacific without returning home.

In many ways, Mills's 'Frank Leman' and 'Edwin Florance' are alike. Mills uses epigraphs and chapter divisions, stereotyped characters and situations, and local dialect in each. Both share an aura of fantasy, although Mills protests of 'Frank Leman': 'The incidents which is here Narated is from real life.' But 'Frank Leman' demonstrates much more vividly and completely what must have been the subject of many whalemen's more innocent daydreams.

The hero, Mills's 'chum,' takes a vacation to hunt, fish, and read in the country. Frank is deferred to by everyone, stays at a homelike inn which serves an abundant and varied lunch twice every day, and is surrounded by orchards filled with fruit for the taking. For whalemen, condemned to an appallingly monotonous diet, with fresh fruit especially at a premium, this is a dream setting indeed – all the more so as the hero is elevated from second mate on a whaling ship to wealthy Cantabrigian.

In addition to all its other attractions, the setting offers an abundance of beautiful, charming, virtuous – and well-to-do – young women. Mary Howard is the prize of all. Most beautiful, most charming, and most virtuous, she is the apple of her rich parents' eyes. When Frank saves her from drowning, they fall in love and marry soon after. The story closes with a report of Mr. and Mrs. Frank Leman's happy married life. No doubt the most satisfied reader of 'Frank Leman' was John Martin, who watched his own fantasies unfold in his friend's journal.

Mills's 'Preffatory Remarks' observe a common literary convention, asserting that the novel is based on fact, that the author was present during some of the scenes, and that details have been changed to prevent readers from recognizing the actual setting.

AN ETERNITY OF LOVE

Frank Leman, Or: A Month. in the Country

By the Author of
Edward Merwin or Life in Kentucky
The Pirate Schooner –
Ines De Isturbile or the Young Pioneers
George Bertram or the Revenger and the Avenger
Etc Etc Etc Etc Etc Etc Etc
George. Edgar. Mills. Leut
United States Martime

Preffatory Remarks to Novel No. 6th

The incidents which is here Narated is from real life. some parts of which the Author himself. was a person interested. to some considerable extent. As for "Leman. (a ficticous name,) he was the Authors most intimate Friend and companion. in fact. what may be called {a chum} the scenery would if traced by those that reside in that section be recognised if described as it actually is therefore a little embelishment is nesessary. if any Mistakes are found I most humbly beg the reader to excuse them. But what is lacking in wit and Prosey eoulogies must of course be laid to its originator

Yours Sincerely
G. Edgar Mills
U. S. Maritime

Ship Leonidas
March 4 1856

Chapter First

hurah – high cliffs, ye Crags and peaks,
I'am with you once again,, Payne,

Can you. direct me to the Hotell, my little man, said our hero, to an urchin, one fine Morning In June, of No great date past.

Yees Sir; I'll tell you. yer see that ar pole sir, all streaked round. like candy. wall that's whar "Joe" Barbers is. yer go on, and turn round whar yer see. a golfired big Mortor pestel. stuck up before Doctor Jenney's store. right close to his'in youll see the tavern, ef thats whar yer want ter go tu

Thank you, my boy, here is a ten-cent piece for you. said Frank.

Thank ye sir. am yer going to live 'ere sir, said the boy looking wistfully at the piece of Money, and then at Frank.

Frank replied by snaping his, shay up. leaving the boy rich with his ten cent piece.

Frank. drew up at a fine looking little Building. which bore the sign of the Grafton House everything looked neat. and well to do. and as he resigned the reins to the ostler. the Host. made his appearance full of life and with a, good morning Sir a fine morning for a ride. will you walk in sir. Jim see to the Gentlemans horse a carrige. walk in sir, walk in. sir. and he was bowing and looking as obliging as possible.

Landlord said frank. seating himself in the little back parlour. Can you furnish me with a room. A nice pleasant one mind., for a few days, perhaps weeks. I like the looks of your house and things about. and. and of yourself and Lady. so if you can accamadate me I shall stop and enjoy myself here. for a few days

Lord Bless you sir. exclaimed the Host Ben Norton. by the way. enthusiastically you've come to Jest the place sir for pleasure. The plea of Franks took. And continued Ben. I pride myself of being Just the Man, to make everybody enjoy themselves, that comes here sir. Anything thats wanting, sir, is at your service, will you look at your Room sir. motiong towards the door

Frank: Thank. you Landlord. I know I shall like your mode of living, like your rooms, like your Family. In fact Landlord I shall like everything here providing you've got good Fishing. good Hunting. and fine old forests to ramble through O Landlord. I shall require so many things which Nature. and the Industry of Man cannot produce that you will call me an excentric rattle-headed scape grace. By the way Landlord is there plenty of Berries, wild ones I mean. plenty of Apples. of plumbs, cherries, peaches, pears and above all is there any pretty girls to romp with eh. LandLord.

Land.: Why my dear sir. what a string you run on. to be sure. Bless your soul theres a Gentleman last summer that stoped 'ere two months an, he said he never took so much regular right down rollick fun in all his life past I assure you. and for fishing or hunting I calculate there amt any. woods. or rivers. any where round these diggins, that for. game. or fine old places to sit down an read a book now and then in. as there is in Grafton. although I say it sir 'taint to be beat. Then for Apples an that ere. kind of fruit there's thousands of it sir. that Lays on the ground all winter. all for want of some one to pick it up. and as for girls. Whew. you wait till sunday. if you want to see a sight. There's Sarah Spaulding. there aint a fellow in the place but what would Jump alf way up to the moon for a kiss. an theres Nance Holt. a sprightly. Blue eyed, Mery hearted gal, that everybodys in love with her. There's Sally Jones a better mans. wife than she would make, never lived. and there's Alice Burk. and there's Jenny Clark, and there's Ellan Powers, and there's Nelly Blake. and oh ever so many more, thats first rate girls. But I must tell you about one, her Name is Mary Howard. –

Mary Howard. thats a pretty name –

"Tis so. my dear Sir. and the name was never owned by a prettier girl than she. an she so kind to everybody. and so gentle. and Loving to her old parents. tis a blessing to them. such a blessing as few parents possess. every body says she's an angel or as near as can be. why sir. She's every where amongst the poor. – and many a couch of sorrow and sickness has she soothed down for the sufferer. Not a poor family in the Village. Sir. but what has cause to bless the Name of Mary Howard. –

Well – well. Landlord. but where does this angel of yours live, how far from here.

Well sir. I should say its a short half a mile to Squire Howard's or there-abouts. He lives in a Large wood building. all surrounded with fine old Maples. that stood there for over forty years as I can swear too. he's got a large Farm. and the best one too. around. 'ere. and he's so kind and good natured old soul. that every body thinks everything of him. He's the best. and richest man in these parts sir. but, my dear sir, I'm afraid I'm troubbleing you with my gossip. so I'll take myself off you can see square Howards. from this 'ere window and in fact sir. you can see a great many things that will give you pleasure. when you've been 'ere a little while. – and if you – There + if I hain't been keeping you here. till its Luncheon time as the clock is Just struck ten. an we always eats Luncheon twice a day.

I should think it a verry good plan; especily to get 'rid of your coald vituals, Landloard

'Tis so sir. but – ef – em – you'd call me 'Ben. sir. what every body calls me. it would sound more like home. and be more – em – be more – like – excuse me sir. like Friendship:

Chapter Seccond

. . her cheeks were like. the.
Roses. that spontaneously Bloom.

"*Higho. two days in the country and not an adventure yet. soloquised. Frank . . L . . . n one fine morning. two days subsequently to the Last.*

'*This speaks well for you young man. and contradicts the character, I left at old P . . . . s school However. I'll soon make it up. here I bee. and I'll sport if such a thing is in my powre This old Gun. I supose will find me a little sport till along into the afternoon and then what shall I do. Oh Dear Me. ah here's Gulivers travels. I'll take that along it may make up for luck. I wonder who that young female was that I see going acrost the fields yestardy what a quick and graceful step she had. and how charmingly she executed the maneuver of jumping the stone, wall. ha. ha. ha. how I should have like it, to have seen Julia, or Ellen, Nelson, a Jumping the fence: ha. ha. by Jove, I'll bet they'd come down one half on one side and one on the other. then shouldn't I like to have offered my help to extricate them. Just at that turn. Well, I suppose experience learns everything almost. and so it would be with them, in a little while no doubt. What! eight oclock. I'de ought to have been in the woods long ago. better late than never. and with that he shouldered his double team! as he used to call his fowling peice, and mosied! for the woods.*

His luck was not much, in fact he did not try verry hard. so after an hour. or so. he sat down on a log by the side of a deep and placid river, some mile or so from the village. he resorted to the more profitable work of amusement. that of reading.

How long he had been thus occupied, he had no Idea. but was startled by a scream. so wild! so shrill and piercing. that it almost. raised his heart to his mouth. as it was, he Jumped from his seat. dropping his Book, droping his gun. and hat. and raised his eyes toward the sound. he saw a sight! that for a moment. Paraglised, every faculty.

About. two Hundred Yards. above where he stood the bank, rose high and overJutted the under part of the bank. on the verge there grew a few raged alders. and on to these bushes. there hung a female. he comprehended all in a glance! she had steped out to the top of the bank. and the earth caving off she barely saved herself from being precipitated in the water. by grasping these shrub alders. and there sent out that thrilling note of alarm. which so astounded Frank"

AN ETERNITY OF LOVE

It needed no seccond. glance for him to determine his proceedings. He sprank with the quickness of thought. to her rescue. it was but the work of an instant to brace himself against the roots of the alders, with the danger of falling into the river with her he was trying to save.

"Dear Lady! be not alarmed. there rest your arm, on my shoulder. thus. now let go! I've got you fast. you cannot. fall! dont be afraid. there step here! Now then. Dear Lady. thank god you'r safe. you had a narrow escape but for those freendly bushes. –

– And you, my preserver. I now should. perhaps been lifeless. O how can I ever repay you. or sufficently attest my gratitude to you. O. thanks! a thousand thanks! for your prompt assistance. and. –

No. No. Dear, Lady, I need no thanks for doing what any Man. would do. but lean on my arm. you are weak and exhusted therefore with your permission. I will see you safely home.

O. thank you sir. I do indeed feel weak. and exausted. if you will help me home. a Fathers. Thanks. and a mothers. blessings shall in some Measure speak for my sincerity.

You prize my assistance to highly. but sit down one moment if you please. on this stone while I regain my hat. and a few other things which I dropped on seeing you. hanging by those bushes.

It is not far. so compose yourself. I shall not be gone but a few moments. and away he went. after his. hat.

It took him but a short time to accomplish his object but in that short time the Maiden, had recovered herself from her fright, but she blushed and hang down her head as she met Frank's looks of admiration. Never before had he seen so Lovey a form and countenance. as she timidly enquired if he had succeeded in finding his hat. poor soul. she did not know what she was saying. for if she had looked on his head she would have seen it. but Frank, he was to much of the Gentleman to keep a fair. maid long. in such confusion. he gently offered his arm. and she! tremblingly gave her white and delicate hand to frank. who gently drawed it through his arm. and away they started for home.

I hope you. did not hurt yourself. when you caught those Friendly shrubs. – did you –

O no sir. not in the least. but I was teribly frightned. and oh. how glad I was when you so fortunately hove in sight. words cannot express one half the thanks. sir, thats your due. but may I know to whome I'me indebted for my life . . . without being inquisitive.

cAND THE WHALE IS OURS

O certainly. my Name is Frank. Leman. I am a student at Cambridge Colledge. and come up here for to spend the vacation. But will you favor me with your name. if —

My Name o. yes. tis Mary Howard sir I live in yonder white house. I had been to carry some fruit to Mrs Hart when you so fortunately saved me.

But are you not some relation to Mr George Leman of Grafton. Mr. Leman. yes. he is my Uncle. but I had entirely forgotten that he lived here, and does he reside far from your residence. Miss Howard.

O No sir. he lives Close too. in fact he is what we call next door Neighbor to us. I am very intimate with his daughter Amy Leman. I congratulate you. Mr Leman. on having so fair a cousin. she's one of the best Ladies I ever was acquainted with. But here we are almost home . . and there's Mother looking out of the Chamber window. oh little does she dream how near I came being drowned. if she did. — "There she sees us. coming. oh he will not bite sir. here Carlo! Carlo! down sir. down. why sir he seems to know you already.

He's a verry pretty dog Miss Howard. he's a water spanlel is'nt he.

yes sir. we've had him ever since he was two months old. But come in sir. I'll take your Hat. if you please. Now please excuse me a moment sir. and frank was alone in the prettiest little parlour imaginable.

The furniture was of the prettiest form not. heavy Mahogany. but neat and pretty. There was a Sofa. which overlooked on a front forest from the window. as you sat or reclined thereon you raise the window on a fine June morning. and a gush of Melodious Music such as Warbling birds can only give would strike your ear and bring calm and Peacefull thoughts home to each

True it was. our hero. perceved those and appreciated them at once. whilst he sat surveying this beautiful retreat the door opened. gently and Mary. accompanied by her Mother entered. Frank. rose as he perceived the Ladies and acknowledged Mary's presence with a light smile, whilst she advanced and taking his hands said with a bright smile said Mr. Leman. allow me the pleasure to make you acquainted with My Mother. Mrs. Howard, this is the Gentleman. and her voice grew tremulous. that saved your Daughter from a watery grave. and — and thank him Mother I cannot thank him for your child's life. and vainly striving to calm her emotion she turned to a window. for concealment.

As for Marys Mother, she extended her hand to Frank. saying, whilst a gratefull smile lit up her frale but cheerfull features. Believe me Mr Leman.

AN ETERNITY OF LOVE

I acknowledge us all your debtors and if I fail in making the acknowledgements to you for bravely. rescuing my child from death. it is because a Mothers heart is to full for utterance. –

My Dear Madam. I assure you. you attach to much importance to an act of duty, for surely it must be less than Manly not to try a rescue seeing a lady in the like situation. I done no more than duty required and believe dear Mrs Howard, the satisfaction I feel in having been of service to your Daughter more than repays me for any trouble I might have been put to. Therefore Madam please say no more of it or realy I shall begin to think I've done something worth complimenting upone and you Fair Maiden I hope will not suffer any inconvenience or indisposition from your late danger. but it is drawing late And if you will be so kind as to direct me to Mr George Leman who is my Uncle I will bid you good afternoon.

But. surely you will stop to supper with us. said Mrs Howard with true Yankee Hospitality at least, do not go, 'till Mr. Howard's. arrival. which will be soon.

No Madam. you must realy excuse. I am as you see a stranger in this part of The country consequently tis best I find my way home before night. or at least to find my Uncle's residence.

O. that you can easily do. for tis not scarce a quarter of a mile there. But if you will not stay with us no longer now. you must promise to call upon us soon.

It will give me the greatest pleasure if I may be so permitted. Beleive me. dear Madam. an acquaintance. so Beautifully began I will not by any means let an opportunity pass by without improving it

Then you will call tomorrow. if your time will permit.

certainly. said Frank. with the greatest of pleasure.

but. if you will Please show me the way to my Uncle's. – O. yes I had forgotton all about it. Mary. will you show Mr Leman the house. Now Mr Leman I shall look for you certainly tomorrow.

I shall not fail. So Good afternoon Madam Good afternoon sir. and with a warm smile and Gentle nod. she closed the door, and went about some household duties whilst Frank and Mary took their out through the Garden. to a little gate at the farther end of the Garden. and upon opening it a well trod path showed itself leading to the right. and in the quiet shade of the Grove beyond could be seen just the top of a white farm house with its customary out door

AND THE WHALE IS OURS

Buildings Frank still holding Mary by the hand. whilst she pointed out the direction. She smilingly added. 'and you will. be sure to call upon us to-morrow. I am sorry that there is nothing verry attractive in our quiet town. to Men who come here for recreation from the city. I am afraid you will find it quite dull here without you can take pleasure in Farming.

O. I think not. I am sure of one thing I shall not look for things more attractive than the acquaintance of sweet Mary Howard you are verry kind. sir. to estimate my poor self so highly. indeed sir I must call that Flatery.

Nevertheless. believe me. Miss Howard it comes from my verry heart. Nay. it is not flattery. it is giving my thoughts to one who I hope will believe me when I say tis sincerely spoken.

"well. indeed I hope we shall not quarrel on that subject said she smiling. but I am realy afraid if you do not look for more attraction than what you will find in me you will be for leaving us soon. saying. perhaps to yourself. tis a dull and lonely village.

No. No. Miss Howard. never. I do not know why I throw my thoughts on your attention seeing that but a few short hours has elapsed since our Acquaintance first began. yet you must forgive me if I intrude to far.

O. certainly. you know we folks of the country are not verry apt to take offence where none is meant which I am sure is not the case. with you.

Then you will allow me to call and see you sometime.

By all means. indeed. I know that my parents would be verry glad to see you verry often.

And would not you be glad to see me too –

yes – that is – you must not – I should like verry well – that is – but Mother will be expecting me so Good Night. Good night and before Frank. hardly knew where he was he found himself alone. He turned round and wended his way slowly towards his uncle's where he arrived in abouts fifteen minutes walk. He was welcomed with all the warmth that characterizes our sturdy and hale old Farmers. and with all the affection that a beloved Brothers Child could expect.

AN ETERNITY OF LOVE

Chapter third

"Tarleton, The thing is settled and – and –
"Seymour." And I am a Happy Man.

O. Father. such an escape to day. I came so near being drowned. twas my own carelessness but. if twas not for Mr Leman's prompt and timely assistance. I should haveve suffered for it. too you cannot imagine. Dear Father. how near I was to.——

Eh. wats that you say. Drowned Eh. how where – where was I. how is it. I dont half understand it, come. why dont you tell me Mary.

"well now then. Father. and she slipped her arm through his. whith such tenderness that the old man smiled so fondly so Lovingly on that fair. round countenance upturned faice and gave a gentle pressure of her arm that smiling swetly she said well now then Father dear I will tell you all about it as we go towards the house. you see. feeling verry tired and lonely I thought I would take a few things over to poor Mrs. Taylor –

Good Girl. my own Mary.

and – and she went on and gave a full recital of all she had gone through with that day. as she ended she gazed up to her Fathers face and saw how pale he looked. she grasped his arm more tightly and exclaimed. what is the Matter ; speak dear Father. what makes you look so pale. oh –

'Tis nothing Mary. my own dear Child you must take care of your self for if you should get killed. oh. 'twould be to much for my old heart to bear God Bless. him for rescuing thee my Child. and he pressed a kiss so fondly on her pure white brow Thank you. Father. dear. I knew you would be gratefull to him for saving. my poor self. but you do look realy ill. has anything caused you trouble. you look pale. oh. so white. –

No. No. Child. I felt startled to think you came so near being drowned. but come let us go to the house. and talk this over with your Mother.

The truth was. the old man was excited and loving his daughter as he did with all the affection of a Father. if he felt a sickness come over him as the startling news was revealed to him and. hence. the paleness of the old Gent.

time passed on and need I add that under the impression first formed. Frank, was a constant visitor at the residence of Mr. Howard's. in fact he was a welcome one in more instances than one if scenes and circumstances are *to be called into question – for in less than a Month. a short. Month he led a happy victim to the Alter. at old Father Fays church. at Grafton. and Mr. & Mrs. Frank Leman one verry fine day took a last look of the scenery and surrounding hills that environed Grafton preparatory to a visit to the ever Famous city of B. . . . . and they are often found Lovingly conversing on the romantic Introduction they had received. and in a look back on the past. Frank is led to exclaim. that of all his pleasure parties he never enjoyed himself with the after peice untill he spent – a Month in the Country[21]*

The most ambitious work on any subject in all the journals is Ambrose Bates's novella of an Eskimo woman's struggle to revenge the slaying of her lover. Writing in 1867–1868, while the *Milwood* was frozen in the ice of Cumberland Sound, Bates had ample opportunity to observe Eskimo folkways, and much of the story is consistent with Eskimo lore and tradition. Bates appears to have mingled what he learned of local Eskimo behavior with more widely known, indeed almost universal, folklore motifs, most particularly that of the scapegoat. On this voyage Bates had moved up to a first mate's berth. As before, he had the time – and the privacy – to compose at length.

The story itself is a tale within a tale. The narrator chances upon an explorer's diary, which sets the scene. Then, 'through other channels,' the narrator continues a highly structured tale, relying heavily on the techniques of melodrama. Note especially the noble hunter and the femme fatale, the fatal promise, the chain of death, the general recurrence of three, the curses, the feuds, the use of flashback, and the philosophical remarks of the 'it was ever thus' variety. Yet Bates's heroine, with the extraordinary name of Tookalooky, is a rare example of a character who manages to rise, if only briefly, above sensational diction and the comic effect of her name. Tookalooky is also one of the few women in all the journals who is described at length.

If we should look upon the map of the world. or rather the great Northern world We should see in Lat 65 and Long 65 the entrance to Cumberland Inlet Then glanceing along past the southermost head-land we see the bay of New Gumemtre. which is partly open to the sea and partly surrounded by a country of Islands Among these Islands a a shifting tribe of Indians very near

AN ETERNITY OF LOVE

resembling the Esquemaux race The few facts which I shall narrate will be of this tribe and which will become connected with a more northern tribe.

Twas when the curious world were feeling for a NW passage that the Heckly and [Fury?]²² two English Exploreing vessels were laying in Fox channel frozen in the ice that a party was made among the more adventuous to cross the channel and enter the interior upon the northern shore A diary of one of the officers which I have here before me runs as follows.

Jan 5th After refreshing ourselves and dogs we steered as near North as the uneavness of the country would admit After passing through low leaded some 20 miles we again came to ice which we cut and found to be salt water. Here we were met by an old native with his ogjog and toggle for sealing. With a short conversation between him and our guide he leed off until we rounded a point in the land whire we cane upon a settlement whire sone natives had taken up their winter quarters Here were sone 30 tupicks or igloes and perhaps sone 200 natives

There arose some strife between the differant families who should be honored by keeping one or two of the party. Sayes the writer It fell to my lot to be the guest of an old man and his son, wife and daughter.

The first evening of our so journe I discovered that several young men were there off and on through the evening But on the seccond day I learned that there excisted a jealousy between two young hunters for the favor of the daughter of mine host Whose name was Tookalooky.

Tookalooky was a damsel of some fifteen or sixteen summers. with a beauty scarcely surpassed by by the great nations of the civilized world. In her own country she would be called tall. But were she a native of New England she would be called below the medium statue Her eyes as a characteristic of the race must be very dark But in this instant there lurked a milder beam. which softened the wild expression so natural among those people Her round full features and the freshness of her complection distinguished her from all others in that desolate country

Young Eban Tuker a stout athletic young hunter has grown up with her childhood and of all others was the one she most esteemed. And although Peter Hungerman (another young hunter) very often called upon her still she could not use the familliarity with him as with her old acquaintance. Therefore Hungerman was filled with a jealous hatred for (as he supposed) the only obsticle between himself and the fair Tookalooky. At last a mutial hatred *grew up between those two lost sons of Iseral And often when hunting the Iwick or Netchuck or on the trail of the poler bear these two men would meet and turn from each other as two infinite powers*

Twas summer and Ebantuker had completed an Iglo of his own and gained the consent of her Father Ardordar to take the lovely Tookalooky to ocupy this new habitation

But Paterhungerman now came fourth (as he claimed) a promis fron her Ardardor to be fulfilled

I should have stated that Paterhungerman was ten years older than Tuker and twelve older the the fair Tookalooky. And when the damsel was but a child of six summers She strayed from the settlement or squating ground And after a long search in vain there were several bears discovered lurking about as though they had tasted some sweet morsel to attract them to prolong their stay And the little girls parents in their dispair had offered to any one who would rescue her not only the girl as an adopted daughter but All the 2(deer Skin whiren their weath cosisted) Tooktook skin in their possession. Hungerman was the lucky individual who returned the child unharmed to her parents. Whireupon he had recieved the tooktook skins but being a young single man did not care for the child and willingly gave up his claim

But now in this last hour has come forward to claim that which eaven though the Father were willing to acceed he has no more the power to do so

Eban Tuker now being accainted with the demand upon his affianced. demanded that he should give over his claim and forever announce all intentions that he should have ther or there after upon one who was the affianced bride of another

Hungerman departed with uttering one word but with a threatning gesture draged himself as though reluctantly from them. That Night Tukar went out and his long absence soon called others to enquair for him but in vain until Aeshiph [?] lit upon the dead form of the young hunter with Hungerman's speer yet remaining in his body

The deed was looked upon with silent horrow in this country of no laws. Though no one steped forth to revenge so horible a deed still the man of blood shrunk from his own preasance. Nor ever dared to look to Tookalooky again eaven as a friend

So ends the tale of the explorior and there I through other channels resume the consequences which led from that tragedy

AN ETERNITY OF LOVE

Haveing been several years among the Esquimaux tribe upon the Assiatic coast whire I picked up a few words of their language And several more on the shores of Davis Straits. Spending several winters among them I became comparitvely well informed in their language In the winter of 1855 I became to know a native far advanced in years. And which learned formerly belonged to the Newgumeuke tribe It now being 1857 and our good ship Milwood frozen in the ice in Cumberland Inlet²³ I took a curiosity to question the same old native spoken of above which is here lveing with his sail [?] And through him I am able to continue the above Narative

Hungerman the homicide after the accomplishment of his hellish deed wandered away frm his former companions with his load of guilt whire he should no more as he thought meet the gaze of a scorning world And for several years thought himself secure from all observation

In the meantime young Tookalooky had her every sense bent on revenge for her murdered lover And though a female she laid her deep and shure

When she first saw her affianced waltering in his gore. her sensibilities were sensibly affected and for a while gave way to sad lamentations

Which soon passed off and she resumed a composure that our greatest phylosophers should have been commended for. Her nature soon retained its lvely cheerfulness and it seemed with her as it naturaly was with others less interested. That is as though naught had transpired to break the monotony of the times

But still there lurked that deadly hatered for the offender that could only be appeased with blood.

As Tookalooky was beautiful (which is the magnet which man so raedily answers to its attractions) had not long to wait before a score those infatuated being were sighing for a place in her affections

And she with an ever scheeming heart encouraged all and faned their infatuations with such a condecending grace that all seem to think that a shure conquest was for him And thus matters remained until she her self should get some clue to the runaway murdier Listning to every [?] hunting excursion. That she might get some clue to a strange trail

One day a party of hunters haveing returned were surprised to find that none beside had left the settlement since their departure as they had seen fresh marks upon the [sic] indicating that some individual was near whire they had spent the previous night Though at the moment there were some wonder who or when those marks being too. but with a simple solution of the matter it ended At least so it seemed But there was one that gladly treasured up the seeming trifling mysteries And that night she baffled the allurement of the God of Slumber to cherish a hope which she had begun to dispair of ever realiseing

For severel times during that long winter ther were reports of strange trails and none knew or felt the shirety that Tookalooky did of the real author of those marks

With all the caution of her nature did she proceed in that revenge. her every desire had long dictated Though she regreted to see her victim so long at large comparatively enjoing his freedo yet she comforted herself to think how heavy would be the blow when he becone reconciled to his secluded life. whilst evr assurance of his safty had become seemingly a matter of course But little did he dream there was one that as yet had never ceased to cherish the most revengeful desires to see him brought to an eaqual horred end as the one whose blood he had spilt

Among her suiters were several whom the damsel had encoaraged to almose an surety And these three young hunters looked upon each other with a jealous eye as they beheld the regard Tookalooky paid to each in their preasance At last one summers day when there were great preparations throughout the settlement e'er they should strike tents and disperse to the different parts of the country in their long anticipated deer season On one of these days it was reported that Tookalooky was lost and in a few minutes these young men flew to her rescue. Of a matter of course she was found by one of these and him she told a startling tale of abduction

As she was by a brook by the settlement dressing some Nitchuck Hungerman made his apperance and before she could give the alarm she was stifled with a deerskin covering which he hove over her head. Then she was boarn away wheather she could not tell Neather could she have an idea how long nor how far she was carried in this way. She haveing lost all conciousness But for what length of time she could not tell And when at last she was restored to conciousness she found herself in the company of the above named gentleman who professed all the love of former time. But she shrinking from him. he at last got angry and threatened a dreadful revenge in case she would not leave all and share his unsocial fortunes She feigning an acquiesance watched her chances for escape From him she learned that they were some 20 miles to the eastward of the settlement and on the second day whilst Hungerman was off *in quest of game of which they were greatly in need of she made her escape and had at last found here way to the place where she had been met by this young man And now she took the opportunity to inform those three young men sepperately that she could not think of becomeing the wife of anyone as long as this man should infest the country and if she could be assured that he was no more she would then feel at liberty to make an engagement with her chosen one. Intimateing at the same time that the one preasant was the one best beloved.*

As a matter of consequence each one of those infatuated lords set his brain to work to hatch up some plan whereby measures could be taken to rid the land of this outlaw. And though each felt a horrow of staining his own hands with the blood of the victim still each had a lurking desire to appear in the eyes of Tookalooky that they were the sole instigtors of the affair which she so much desired to see executed

At last summer came and with the dispersion of the differant fammilies to the different hunting grounds in quest of deer

Tookalooky telling her devoties the she should remain at the old island anxiously waiting to hear of some ones account of the death of Hungerman. Those three young men which I will name as they are here spoken of so often Their ages were all near the same. The first or largest was named Abbeluclook. The seccond Parcok The third Ocakokjo. These three were seperated in differant parties and during the summer at different times each one of them fell in with the trail of the wanderer of which each made it his business not to loose sight of And finely Ocalokjo and Abbelooktook comeing togather disclozed their designs and found they both were on the same errent of blood with the same prize in view. and instead of denounceing the scheemer. boath commended her for her master hand at seeking the life of him who had abducted her away from the settlement as they believed. And thes tow young braves concluded to through their chances togather and win the fair one by striking the first blow And many a day did they seek this trail expecting each new morn to achieve the greet end One day in August they past a smouldering fire which seened had been lighted but a few hours before And so they presed on in hopes of overtakeing its kindler eer another nigh should frustrate the trail which now seemed so plan and shire But night came down and as they could not proceed with any ceartainty concluded to wait the comeing daylight But in the larter part of the night they espied a light beside a distant mountain

They did not wait any longer but horred toward it. But the differculty of traveling in the night and the distance being so much farther than they antici- pated they did not reach the place until after daylight As they now were near enough to see a human being thought it more prudent to come in on boath sides of him and therefore the one continued whire they then were whilst the other advanced eround a hill and then boath were to advance simaltanously upon their victim But judge of their disappontment as they with rifle leveled at their expected foe. to behold in its place their friend Parcok And much more to astonish them he was leaning over the corps of the Homicide Pater Hungerman who he with his own had had killed. And also judge of his surprise when the three mutialy opened their hearts and found that each had been sent on the same bloody errent by Tookalooky with the same assureances of her regards

Not as rivals of the more enlightened did those misled swain deal with each other But here upon the spot did they pledge themselves to forsake the vene- mous charmer. And in consort did the sever from the body of their victim the gastly featurs and returning they with one accord presented sam to Tookalooky

One moment only they paused to gaze upon the vengful sadisfaction which seemed to settle upon her countinence Then turning away left her to her own deep thoughts Each resolveing to see her no more

It matters little to this tale whatever became of that revengeful daughter of eve Although she had fiengned to love the three young men before mentioned yet that sentiment turmed love had died from her bosome when she saw the object of her first affection carried from a bleeding murdered corps

She since had nursed a feeling for revenge and since that propensity had been staciated it seemed that her mission in this world had been fathfully preformed and now her work was ended

Wheather any one ever wooed or sued for her hand I know not But it is ceartain she never was bound with bons of matrimony and died at an advanced age

But not so with poor parcok for in extripateing the homecide he himself became one nearly as detested Which I will in the sequel show

The capture and final destruction of Hungerman was soon known through- out the place. And as the very name of the murderer had become a fear through their superstition Of cours all must rejoice at being relieved of such a pest. And with the first impuls Parcok was applauded by all as the deliverer

AN ETERNITY OF LOVE

And thus time roled on and Hungerman was comparately forgotton. But not so the one whose had had delt the finishing stroke. But gradualy and impreceptibly there grew a superstitious fear of Parcok. And eaven the children caught the infection. and would shun him as some ferocious beast. And this Parcoks triumph He had never taken a wife but a sister of his who was partially blind had done his work and lived in sometimes one and sometimes another iglo just as accomodations would admit But at last None would keep him. And so he build a small place of his own and he and the described old maid live a solitary life. No one ever called upon him and if perchance he had occation visit a neighbour he was eyed as though an expectant knife was ready to cleave the heart of any one who should happen to be back to in his preasance

Still he must hunt over the same grounds Wander over the same fields of ice in quest of Nitchuck. And paddle his kiac over the same waters And as superstition has ne er been known to subside. But on the contrary it needs must buld itself up until some great reaction must take place Now at last it became noised about that eaven the game on which they depended for subsistance forsook the ground on which he trod And the waters oer which his kiac went. At last the whole settlement was destroyed and the people with one accord saught to make their new camping ground far from the haunts of Parcok But no sooner had they settled in their new abode. Then Parcok came and built also himself an iglo by himself. though within half amile of the others. How unnatural it is for man to be alone. Now this man of nature although he knew that he was detested still rather than be so ceartainly alone he rather choose to be within the vacinity of his enemies.

When it became known at the settlement that their new hunting grounds was to be subject to Parcok. And that superstitious fear which come over all again stired their peace and so they called a meeting and concluded to rid the country of such a pest. All agreed that was the only thing now left to be done And though the meeting held to a late hour. How no who should strike the blow was not mentioned. Wheather it was alluded to or not in their own minds shure no are perpared the subject

Although I have remarked how scheeming the maiden Tookalooky was. I will now on the other hand remark what simplicity we find in the counsil of those brave hunters It would seem that although all agreed that the man must be removed yet the simple idiea did not occur then that any there must or could perform the deed.

And so the assembly disperced with a general understanding that the man must be – what – killed – Husbands told their wives that he was to be killed. Sons told their mothers the same story And soon all told the same story and the fact was established and strange as the proceedings were it was promptly executed. As if some higher will then mans was superintending the whole affair. and one of these men run unconciously into his own snare

Parcok haveing become accostomed to his outcast life was content to know that he lived and mooved in common with those neighbours which detested him. He and his sister who lived in and took care of his iglo seemed to enjoy themselves somewhat. That is as far as any one could tell

One afternoon Parcok was returning from a hunt loaded with the spoils of the chase and as though chance would have it so he came upon a party of hunters who were also returning from a hunt though an unsuccessful one Parcok no sooner percieved with what success his brethern had spent the day and freely offered to share his gains with them and spread his load out before them And their sharpened appertites forbade their refusals And after haveing helped themselves to a harty meal they all started on their journey homeward togather All talking of the verious incidents of a hunters life & untill they came to the point whire the homeward path led contrary ways. And as Parcok singled out on his path alone dreaming not of danger. On the contrary feeling sadisfied within himself that he had done one good act to his brethern. which they would give him credit for and perhaps be more united toward himself

But loo to repay his act of kindness he beholds them standing watching him with their weapons ready for action He too paused when seeing their threatning attitude and laid down his load not believeng he himself was the meditated victim One of the three Hungryparr by name now deliberately walked up to Parkok with knife in hand and burried it deep in his bosome Parkok now made one effort to escape but again recieveing a cut yealded to his assasen who finished his bloody work with pity The two spectators now made a hasty retreat refuseing to accompany the new murderer to their settlement

Thus we see that Hungryparr had taken the lif of the guilty murderer and at the same time taken the guilt upon his own shoulders. Not only the guilt but he must inherit all the inconvenientcies of a hated outcast And from this instance Hungryparr was transformed from a leading member of the tribe to a forsaken miserable wretch And why should he volunteerly take this great obligation upon himself.

It was the rude instinct of an uncultivated mind It was the lack of that education which more civilized society bestows upon mankind. Mankind is no more nor less than the brute if reared by its natural instinct

Poor Hungryparr has made the great mistake of life which he never will be able to make right again. His fellow men will never forgive a deed which they all was ready to do themselves His fate is sealed for life. Like as an erring women though they entreet the world howe er so penitant they can never be restored to their former favor This is an injustice which cannot be remadied Though we all may pity and eaven desire to replace them to their former position still the heart will instinctive recoil from them

But Hungryparr has no notion of being left behind as Parcok was before him And although he was detested by his own kind still he imagined he could not be without them Hungryparr had a wife and two children. Two little girls who are now of the ages of 9 & 12. The older being blind of one eye. His wife is some forty years old. In his iglo and belonging to his household is another man and a little son of 8 years. Aneticketon is the name of the hunter which ocupies the abode of the outcast.

I am told by the natives here that before the murder of Parcok this Hungryparr was one of the first men among them But now to my knowledge he is just as much degraded as the lowest pauper of our country. He is a noted liare and what ever he will lay his hands upon is shure to appropriate

If there is a dirty job to be done Hungryparr is the first applied to He provides his family with the most disgusting articels the country affords. and these becaus he can obtain them without labour. I have seen his iglo piled up with stale whale meat, foxes, and when a dog happens to be killed. Hungryparr is shure to look after the carkess I haveing engaged his fox skins. have known him to go on board of a Scotch vessel and dispose of one for just half of what I was to give him. just for the sake of telling a falshood and thereby realize the curs which is upon him These people reminds me of the ancient who went foarth to single combat and old feuds continued through several generations

Now there is a youngster growing to manhood whome these people have choosen to avenge the death of Parcok And he seems to acquiesce readily to the proposed arrangement. I asked him if he really should shoot Hungryparr O yes he said when I am a man. And I believe that thought will grow within him untill it is realy a fact. And this goes to proove how essential it is to rear children to ideas of true merit

Now this child of nature believes himself to be the future avenger of Parcok and the champeon of right Little dreaming that the deed no sooner performed then he resumes all the responsibilities which have been the burden of Hungryparr

Not only the boy seems inocent of these facts but the tribe in general seems to think that it would be a great honor to rid the community of such a pest as Hungryparr But the act once executed and these same advisers would be ready to persecute their tool for the very act which they themselves had urged him to do

But time will disclose the end of this line of tragedies Or if Hungryparr should happen to die a natural death before some one relieves him of the burden of life then perhaps the curs which was to be entailed upon the third and foarth generation had found its last victim

So Hungryparr I leave you to fate hopeing none may follow in thy footsteps [24]

Love and simple sexuality inevitably preoccupied many whalemen on long and boring voyages. But they wrote when they were far from women, during an age which severely limited what emotion could be portrayed in print. Of course, more intimate expressions of feeling may have been destroyed, but these examples show how conventionally many expressed their thoughts, even within the privacy of their journals.

The 'Frozen Limb,' unique as it is here, is not truly remarkable. Like William Wilson's confused narration of the doings of the Queen of Otaheite, it is impersonal. Pornography, after all, has its own conventions.

The longer and more technically skilled works are also clearly within the traditions of the time. Mills, it is true, departs from the norm. In an era which delighted in complicated and tumultuous romance, he was capable of writing a simple, happy love story. But although he based his tale on fact, and although his protagonist no doubt guided the telling of the tale, the characters, their emotions, and the plot are all familiar and totally predictable. The particular details that 'Frank Leman' himself could and probably did relate have almost all been omitted.

AN ETERNITY OF LOVE

Bates's Eskimo melodrama, complex as it is, falls even more within Victorian tradition. What gives his material its special interest is his dramatic use of unusual ethnic detail, and his sense of the fatality which pulls the focus of his narrative to the eternal renewal of the cycle of death. In fact, neither Mills nor Bates seems particularly interested in 'Love,' nor in its individualizing specifics. Each simply assumes romantic love as a motive, as a means of initiating or complicating a plot.

It is a remarkable jump from these effusions of emotion to Samuel Braley's detailed and ambivalent analyses of his own feelings. His outpourings, the most personally illuminating of all, examine both his feelings about women in general and his wife Mary Ann in particular. His ability to recognize his occasional real hostility makes his more tender memories all the more credible. His spontaneity rises above the strictures of his society about the emotion proper to his situation. Braley is neither simply a lover nor a misogynist: he is, at different times, both. The contrast, the range, create the sense of a whole person, capable of many feelings, that is absent from the work of the rest of these writers.

Oblivion

Yes age creeps on Bant never mind
The present is near. Distant time
Will bring a day when all our gain
Our costled hopes and boasted name
Are left above an humble grave
Where soon Oblivions mighty wave
Rolls over all Then no one there
If asked could tell we ever were

But man still claimes another sphere
Where time shall rolle Bant bring no seer
To mark decay. An endless year
Shall fill eternal space and bring
That promised life eternal spring
Oblivion then is but a dream
And Lethe too a fabled stream
A land of stories yet unseen

One page of Ambrose Bates's journal, kept on board the New Bedford bark
Milwood, 1868–1869.

CHAPTER FOUR

THE GRIM MESSINGER
OF DEATH

Death was a much more immediate subject for many whalemen than either home or love. Their own lives were often threatened by illness and dangerous work at sea. And, in those early days of medical science, the lives of loved ones on shore were often endangered also.

Shipboard doctoring was unreliable, as many journals reveal. A Yankee whaleship's crew almost never included a trained physician, although doctors occasionally signed on with the crew or traveled aboard for personal reasons.[1] Besides their other responsibilities, whaling skippers were expected to prescribe remedies and, in emergencies, even to perform surgery. A look at a period medical handbook shows how scanty a captain's medical training could have been: half a page on lacerations, a page on amputations, a page and a half on diagnosing signs of death.[2] There is a widespread tale, one can only hope apocryphal, of the captain whose medicine chest bottles were numbered to correspond with those in a handbook of remedies. If the captain ran out of bottle eleven, so the story goes, he simply mixed bottles five and six.

Even if a whaleman survived such treatment and the other perils of whaling life, he might return to find that relatives and friends had died while he was away. Mail and hometown newspapers often failed to reach whaleships, which sailed unpredictable courses. A whaleman could never be sure who would still be alive to greet him.

Death was, understandably, a difficult subject for whalemen to face. Many writers, unwilling to explore a frightening topic for themselves, turned to the ready-made phrases and forms they found in sentimental novels, memorial broadsheets, and newspaper verse to express their feelings. As might be expected, the results were generally trite and awkward. But some writers were more original, as the following examples show.

Most whalemen's writing on death, like most of their creative writing in general, was poetry. Very little on the topic was done by such sophisticated writers as William Macy. Most is simple, filled with the clichés which have always bloomed about the tomb, and modeled on the traditional epitaph.

Henry M. Bonney, a mate on board the *William Badger* in 1847, composed one of the rare prose examples. His address to his dead sister uses most of the well-known themes and images popular among Victorian writers, such as the 'thorny path' of life and the 'grim Messinger of Death.' But despite Bonney's reliance on conventional ideas and phrases, several personal details appear, perhaps because his sister's circumstances in some ways resembled his own. Like Bonney, she left home to live among 'strangers' – in her case, the members of the Mormon church.

My Sister when wee last parted I suppose that neither of us thought the grim Mefsinger of Death would place his icy hand of uppon us to call us hence in to that vast eternity and in to the presance of a hart serching god. But such has been the command and You My Sister have Yealded up your spirit into the hands of your creator and as I trust with Joy & not with grief. Though My Sister pased from time to eternity far from her native home and parental roof I trust She found friends among Strangers iff not Brothers and Sisters in the Bonds of Christ who would Sooth the acheing Brow and cool the parched lip allthough She Differd in Sentiments from Mee and was strong in the Mormon faith I mourn her lofs for Nothing cant Make it good though her path was a thorny one for the Last of her days I trust now it is plesant as the presance of Christ and the holy angels can Make it for did she not Die full of the love of god and love to all the world[3]

George Mills's prose meditation on the sudden and painful death of a shipmate, Andrew Carlton, takes up the often horrifying subject of death at sea.

The Mariner's Grave

"our Shipmate is gone. but he shall not sink upon his watery bier unwept.
G. E. Mills

" The consignment of a frail remnant of clay to the silent tomb. is at all times a dread solemnity. I have seen the simple village train surround the rude bier.

THE GRIM MESSINGER OF DEATH

containing perhaps the companion of thier childhood and pour forth the
Lamentations of heartfelt sorrow. er're they placed it in its narrow cell.

I have heard the solemn and deathlike sound of the muffled drum as it
preceeded some gallant son of Mars. whose sorrowfull comrades were about to
pay him the last tribute of respect.

All these I have seen and witnessing which has filled my mind with feelings
at once Gloomy and sorrowfull. but. tis the burial at sea. when the departed
shipmate or kind loving Friend. enshrouded in his Hammock in which he was
wont to sleep. his cares away. is Launched into the boundless deep. no green
turf to cover his head – no stone to mark his Sepulchre. the piping. North East
wind his Funeral dirge. The sea birds fitfull scream his only requiem; tis at
this time the most hardned of gods creatures. as he sees the dark blue waters
close over the remains of him. who. but a few short days before, perhaps – as
many hours, was joining in the Gambols of the Ship with a spirit as Buoyant
as air. it is at such a time he becomes doubly sensible of death and an life
hereafter.

As the sojourner on shore places the remains of the partner of his bosom. or
the child of his affections beneath the silent earth. he has the gratification.
though a slight one. of viewing the dreary prison that contains them and will
take a maloncholly pleasure in contemplating the green mound beneath which
his kindred or acquaintance is mouldring into dust – but the mariner who
resigns his spirit on the wide and boundless sea. Far – far estranged from home
and country – no fond doating Mother – or loving affectionate sister to close
his sunken eyes or hear the last dying request from his pale and quivering lips.
and when his kindhearted Shipmates. with the briny tear trickling down their
Bronzed and manly cheeks. who perhaps have endeavoured to smoothe his
pillow. towards the conclusion of his mortal race. have consigned him to the
yawning Gulf of the mighty Ocean – one plunge and a slight ripple is all that
remains to tell the resting place of the Hapless wanderer.

Shortly after we left Talchuano. Chile. one of our crew Andrew Carlton. a
noble young Man of twenty five. a native of Georgia, became seriously unwell
the fatal disease} an abscess of the left lung {in a short time made the most
dreadfull ravages in him. and any one to look on that pale and emasiated form
could for a moment beleive it to be the same kind and Gentlemanly Man who.
but a few short months before left Home wife. child – and all to stray away
from them and die. but such is the fell power of sickness. what inroads will it

not make in the Strongest constitutions how will it not unstring the most atheletic and sinewey Frame

After we doubled the cape. he became gradualy worse and worse he sensibly felt his end approaching and resigned himself accordinly. and though everything was done for him that unremitting attendance. and what medical skill the captain possed and the soothing attentions of his Shipmates could do in their anxiety to alleiviate his sufferings. he expired on the seventh of May. 1856

The Eight was a delightfull day. we were mooving along in Gallant trim. with studding sails set and our fine old Bark from the velocity with which she skimed over the Sparkling billows appeared as if to be making up for the adverse winds. and Tempestuous weather. when off the Cape.

And as we hove our ship too with the main topsail to the mast and all hands were called to bury the dead. The tear of sorrow and could be obsereved diming the eye of Many a Gallant sailor standing by. as he perceived the remains of him who. perhaps – had braved with him the dangeres of the perilous deep in youth and Manhood's noblest prime about to be engulphed in a Mariners Grave.

Look upon that Coffin. covered with the Stars of the union. under the flutter of which he who now lays stiffned by the unspairing hand of death. braved the lay [?] terrors of the Poles. or the schorshing influence of the Tropics. and what a subject for Contemplation. Where now is that fond doating wife who at his departure placed the Kiss of affection on his glowing lips looked forward with flattering hopes for his safe return Where now is that fair haired blooming boy. his parents only solace who as he lisps forth the name of his father enquires in thoughtless gaiety when he will clasp him to his fond bossom again. But allas for both he now lies beneath the calm blue waters of the Mighty Atlantic whith the freshening Sea Breeze for his funeral dirge. and the piercing screams of the Sea Birds his only Requiem[4]

Mills's account gains strength from such traditional rhetorical devices as repetition and parallel construction. His catalog of the special torments connected with death and burial at sea is a common feature in whalemen's journals: the absence of a loving family to ease the pains of dying, the unmarked grave which condemns the dead to eternal separation from loved ones at home, and the eerie requiem of bird calls and sea breeze.

John Cleland, Jr., describes a similar burial at sea in verse. Cleland was an unusual journalist. A Wilmington teenager, he was one of several well-bred young members of a debating society who, in a burst of civic pride, signed on for the first voyage of a ship of the Wilmington Whaling Company.[5] But Cleland was clearly unprepared for the rigors of shipboard life, as his journal entries report. This poem commemorates the accidental death of a young Scottish shipmate whose friendship had brightened an otherwise miserable voyage.[6]

... At 4 PM hove the M.T.S. aback the body of the deceased was borne to the gangway the old man read the 96 Psalm. sung the 88th hymn from Dr. Watts book 1st. and read the burial service from the Psalster, we then committed the body to the deep

> *The sun rode high in the cloudless sky,*
> *The Ship oe'r the billows rolled,*
> *When silent and slow we bore from below*
> *The Corpse of our Ship-mate bold.*
> *A while we stood in musing mood,*
> *Then lowered him oe'r the side;*
> *And we wistfully took a parting look,*
> *As he sank in the dark blue tide.*
> *Some bubbles arose from his place of repose*
> *And as quickly forever fled,*
> *We gave but one tear – but that was sincere,*
> *One sigh – for the honored dead.*[7]

Lorenzo Baker, captain of the *Romulus* in 1851, composed a short poem in memory of a crew member who died of consumption.

> *Deep under the green billows deep*
> *On heaps of shell's and sand*
> *Poor Jacob now does lie asleep*
> *Far from his native land*
>
> *He sickened in his berth and died*
> *His friends he'll see no more*
> *For on a plank his corse we laid*
> *And then we launched him o'er*[8]

Later that year, Baker wrote a longer and more ambitious poem about the death of another crew member, this one lost overboard. Quite likely Baker was not only saddened by this death, but also felt responsible as captain for the accidental death of 'the youngest of our crew.' Like Mills, Baker emphasizes the tedium of the voyage, the good qualities of his subject, and the bleakness of the burial scene. Baker uses all the characteristic metaphors: the sea is a coverlet, the coral rocks a pillow, and the waves a shroud.

Lines Written on the Death of Felix Hernon Who was lost overboard from Ship Romulus of Mystic Nov 17th 184 [sic]

We've sailed full many a weary day
We've crossed the burning zone
And still the wild winds round us play
And still we're pressing on
We've passed by many a sea girt isle
And many a rock bound shore
But one who with us welcomed land
Will welcome it no more

He was the youngest of our crew
With bright and sparkling brow
And cheeks of ruddy healthful hue
But Ah where is he now
He sleeps beneath the foaming wave
The coral rock's his pillow
His requiem the howling blast
His winding sheet the billow

One moment full of life and health
We saw him at our side
The next we saw him struggling
In the foaming angry tide
But once he raised his dying head
To see if help was nigh
We strugled hard to lend him aid
But t'was his time to die[9]

J. Goram, a ship's carpenter, sounds a similar note in the first three stanzas of one of his poems. The scene is the same: the endless ocean, the unmarked grave, the requiem in the sounds of the ocean. But his response is strikingly different. The third stanza begins a much less mournful tone. The coral cave is 'bright'; an ocean grave is 'beautiful.' In fact, Goram finds a watery grave infinitely preferable in its beauty, freedom, and brightness to 'cold clods of earth [which] encumber the breast.' His wish for death at sea is unusual.

On the Death of a Shipmate
By J. Goram
Nantucket

Mourn ship mates mourn oh restrain not a tear
Let them fall as a tribute to grace his sad end
For no sculptured marble its head can uprere
To mark the last bed of our Mesmate and friend

Half mast and inverted the Flag of our Nation
As it waves from the Mizzen proclames to the Crew
The rights we are called to preformed and the Ocean
Receieving his Corse excludes it from vew

The Voice of the Sea Bird his requiem is Singing
Whilst low in the depths of the Ocean's blue wave
The music of Sea Shells his death Knell is ringing
And his Corse now inhabits some bright coral cave

How beautiful and bright is the grave of the Ocean
No cold clods of earth encumber the breast
Where the gold fish are sporting and sea plants in Motion
It seems the abode of the happy and blest

May such be my last if my frail bark should ever
By the rude hand of death be Sunk in the wave
When far from my home I am called on to sever
The last earthly tie May Such be my grave [10]

Several writers imitated the highly standardized epitaph quatrains common in newspapers and memorial broadsheets. Standardized in both form and sentiment, these epitaphs leave little room for personal expression. When word of deaths at home finally arrived, months or even years after the fact, whalemen must have been hard pressed to know how to handle the news. Perhaps writing these formal elegiac quatrains brought ritual to deaths that the whalemen could neither witness nor mourn properly.

Captain Orrin (or Orrick) Smalley wrote two of these epitaphs on the death of his mother. In the shorter poem, Smalley recalls his mother's virtuous life.

> Mother dearest of thy kind
> Thy spirit now in peace dost rest
> May thy Children thy precepts mind
> And thus by good acts be ever blefsd
>
> Thou didst us teach the ways of truth
> And now thee's gone to thy reward
> So may thy Children as in youth
> Thy blifsed precepts ever regard
>
> Oft may we think of Mother dear
> And thy memory fonly cherish
> Oft may we drop the silent tear
> For hur who us did nurish[11]

Smalley's longer, less polished poem on his mother's death is somewhat mysterious. The first two stanzas are extremely general, but clear enough. Stanza three is more puzzling: Who is the perpetrator of 'wicked and vain acts'? A family member Smalley is too pained to mention? The poem gives no clue.

> *I*
>
> Dearest mother thou hast gone,
> To that dark and silent tomb,
> The place assigned to the dead
> The which all but Christians dread.

2

Thou was kind and ever good,
May thy Spirit rest with God.
Thy deeds here will ever shine
During man's allotted time,

3

But few there are, as thou hast been,
A mother kind much trouble seen,
My very heart hast oft been pained,
To witnifs acts wicked and vain.

4

But now thy Soule in heaven dwells
Delivered from eternal hell,
Thou wast a Christian here below,
Unto heaven thou wist, to go.

5

Thy Children here will thou remember
Thy memory pricious never surrender,
But try to live, as thou hast said,
And thus obey, our mother dead!

6

May thy spirit an angel be,
Hovering over us in sympathy,
Keeping us from every evil
That we at last may live in heaven.[12]

Another of Smalley's poems, written within two weeks of the others, marks the death of his youngest brother, Isaac. It is very likely that news of these two deaths had reached Smalley in the same letter.

Beloved brother thou art gone
And for the do I often mourn
Thy form wert pleasing to the eye
In a distant land thou didst die

Thy youthful years to me occere
With pleasure sweet do I refur
To days and scenes past and gone
Which we were wont to look upon

Isaac thou wast my youngest brother
And oft for thy fate do I shudder
Did I know thy soul wast at rest
Pleased I should be that thou hadst left.[13]

Captain Angles Snell, writing at the same time as Smalley, also wrote epitaph quatrains to the memory of his mother. Both writers imitated the current fashion in funeral verse (although Snell's skill often falls short in spelling and grammar).

My Mothers Grave,

1. Mother thou has left a wourld of sin
and joined the saints with christ above,
to sing the praises of god's name,
and bask in the glories of his love,

2. Mother thy children mourns thy lofs,
thy loving cairs they cant forget,
and here they place these marble stones,
with loving kindnefs and much respect[14]

Another poem, 'Jane Y. Snell,' takes the same point of view as Samuel Braley's love poem, 'Linger not long – Home is not home without thee': the wife at home speaking her fears to her husband at sea. Was Jane Y. Snell Angles's wife? A sister? A sister-in-law? (He had at least one brother, Moses, also a whaling captain.) Had he just heard of her death? Was he speculating? The poem itself is ambiguous. Perhaps the 'one thats near to me' is a child; perhaps both mother and child died in childbirth.

Jane Y. Snell

O what will my dear husband say
When he returns from sea
And finds that here i lie
And one thats near to me

THE GRIM MESSINGER OF DEATH

> *O tell him I am gone*
> *To regeons in the skyes*
> *He must perpare to meat me there*
> *Whare friendship never died* [15]

A longer and clearer poem Snell calls simply, 'On the death of a yong woman.' The unwitting puns are appropriate.

> *On the death of a yong woman,*
>
> *1 – O sleep deer girl while angels hovers round thy tomb,*
> *thy god has called the home to rest,*
> *my tears shall mosten the green grafs roots,*
> *that groes above thy snow white brest*
>
> *2 – Why should we greave lament and sorrow*
> *since thou art called to a better land.*
> *why should we wish to call the back,*
> *whilts thou arts christ at god's right hand.*
>
> *3 – Why should we feel to wish the here*
> *in this ungratful world of sin.*
> *Should not we feel the change is right*
> *since god has called you unto him.*
>
> *4 – Their is a god that lives above,*
> *that reads aright the hart of man*
> *doth know your life was deer to me*
> *and much to all your earthley friends*
>
> *5 – But since you left us here below,*
> *to dell with christ above the skyes,*
> *their is one here that mourns thy lofs,*
> *and hopes to meet you when he dies,*
>
> *6 – Sleep on deer girl thy sleep is sweet*
> *thy soule's at rest with saints i trust*
> *while beneath the sod thy beautieous fame*
> *lyes moldering in its mother dust.* [16]

But not all the whalemen's writing on death concerned their immediate families or friends. The prolific George Mills turned to a traditional Victorian theme – the orphaned child. As with Bates's 'Grandfathers Story,' it is unclear whether Mills had any personal experience with orphanhood. But again, it may have been a plight easily imagined by a man so far from home and family. In any case, the subject brought out the worst in Mills. 'The Childs Prayer' is filled with clichés and bathos.

> *The Childs Prayer.*
> *By G. E. Mills.*
>
> *Call now on God my gentle boy,*
> *All mortal hope is gone.*
> *Thy dearest earthly friend is dead,*
> *And thou art left alone.*
>
> *The poor boy hears and answers not,*
> *And still the flames roll on.*
> *He thinks of him who came to make,*
> *Each Friendless Child his own.*
>
> *Calm is that brow, serene that heart,*
> *So late with anguish riven,*
> *For God has whispered to that child,*
> *Of happiness and heaven.*
>
> *Again is heard the orphans prayer,*
> *But now in accents mild.*
> *The little Sufferer turns to God.*
> *Oh Father save thy Child.*
>
> *The morning came upon the shore,*
> *Is streached one little form,*
> *Whose face is hallowed with a smile,*
> *Defeant of the Storm.*[17]

Edwin C. Pulver of the *Brutus* was one writer who saw humor in the standard verse epitaph. During 1854 he had written several serious poems in this mode, but soon tired of his work.

THE GRIM MESSINGER OF DEATH

ENough Enough of this great poet
All I can say is let him go it
And when he gets weary of his mother
I hope he I'll speek About his brother

His brother I have Never Seen
And yet I hope he is Not so green
As to rais A song About his mother
For he can Allways find another

Prehaps he might scribble on garden flowers
or of beautiful Nymphs that dwells in some bowers
Formed in the head of the great poet
But one thing is certain he can it ever comest

Prehaps he is scribling to gainst great Nature
And is looking Ahead to the temple of fame
I hope he'll not try so hard as to burst
for of All his workes that would be worst

My right hand is gone. Now I must greive
For the loss of A hand that will Never return
It is A great loss. I can Never retreive
And yet It doath give A lesson to learn

But what was it caused me to strike this blow
That has made me A cripple for life
For long years to come. it will cause me much wo
Un till god calls me from his world of strife [18]

After the grim sobriety of the previous selections, Pulver's 'ENough Enough . . .' will probably please most modern readers as much as it seems to have pleased Pulver. His final stanzas, however, are enigmatic, especially since Pulver's handwriting is consistent throughout the journal.

Two poems on death, surprisingly enough, concerned pigs. Most whaleships carried livestock, and many journals refer to favorite pets (even though they were eventually eaten), the pleasure of eating fresh meat, or the inconvenience of having animal excrement strewn about the deck.

Aside from these two epitaphs, however, livestock inspired few writers to creativity.

Samuel Braley's account of his pet pig's demise is written in both verse and prose.

> *My darling Pigy's back was broke:*
> *For fear that she mte suffer;*
> *I kindly cut her little throat*
> *And had her fried for supper.*

My pet pig fell down the forehatchway this morning and broke her back so we had to kill her; I sorry but I dont think that I shall go into mourning for her. I did think at first that I would not eat any of her; but then I thought that it would be like not getting married again, in case of a defunct Wife; or not excepting a legicy, because your Dear aunt or uncle happened to slip their wind, and leave it to you, so I fell to and Eat her because I loved her – better cooked than raw; and say as people do when they recive a present "I except it for the sake of the giver" the article is nothing of course, especialy in a Ladies eyes, not even a $500 shawl. What nonsence I'm scribling! Good night[19]

Elizabeth Morey, the bride who left Nantucket for the first time with her husband, Captain Israel Morey, wrote the second pig poem. Mrs. Morey's spelling is by far the most eccentric of all the journalists'. 'Critchmas' is one of her more easily recognized distortions, and she uses 'g' at random in most of her journal. Once deciphered, however, her entries, often illustrated, make as interesting reading as any of the whalemen's. The death of the Morey's pet pig, Mr. Hogg, inspired one of her more colorful entries. The form is traditional funeral verse, and the sentiments may be sincere. Chances are Mr. Hogg proved an amiable companion during the long voyage. There is a drawing accompanying the poem entitled, 'Mr. Hogg as I have veiewed on Deck. the last. Eating his corn.'

beging with A Breese from the N.N.E. lotter Part A Briesk Breese with A heavy swell, at 1 oclock P.M. The People on Board Killd the Gogg. Poor Billy A Native of Pits Island, he has Numberd one of our Familey 8 Months and In that time I have got verry much atchaded to him I would go up on Deck. at any time and if he heard My voice he would come to me and ask for his Corn and if I did not take the hint he would pull My Dress or Shall until.

I noticed it and then I would say to him Does Mr Hogg want his Corn. he would answer me. ugh ugh. I think I will draw his likeness

> *Poor Mr. Hogg is Dead, and Gone,*
> *I never shall see him more,*
> *Or hear him beging me for corn,*
> *His loss I do Deplore.*[20]

Another of Mrs. Morey's poems about the death of an animal is happier. It commemorates the death of one of the whales taken by the *Phoenix* – Mrs. Morey named it 'Mercy.'

> *Lovely Mercy we do love thee,*
> *Now your voige of life is O'er*
> *You was the First, Discovered by me,*
> *I shall never Behold you More.*[21]

The poems in this chapter are probably most memorable for their comic effects, whether intentional (as in Samuel Braley's pig poem) or inadvertent (as in Cleland's line, 'some bubbles arose from his place of repose'). Quite obviously, death was a difficult subject to face, either in thought or in verse. While in general the whalemen's verses simply reflect the prevailing social attitudes toward death, it was simple and heartfelt emotion that prompted them to put their thoughts down on paper. Their works may be criticized as being formal, euphemistic, and mawkishly sentimental in the manner of the age, but they still tell us of the peculiar loneliness and tragedy of death and mourning at sea in the nineteenth century.

CHAPTER FIVE

US LONE WAND'RING
WHALING-MEN

As might be expected, whalemen journalists were most concerned with recording what happened around them. And because they were describing their own experiences, the whalemen's accounts of life on board ship make the most consistently interesting reading in the journals. Despite the frequent hazards and hardships of whaling life, most writers turned out sprightly, even celebratory descriptions of their work. But several journalists grew resentful, allowing themselves veiled criticism of the whaling industry in the form of parody, comedy, or satire.

Parody was an extremely popular literary and dramatic form throughout the period.[1] The genre attracted some of the most literate whalemen journalists, four of whom especially stand out: William Macy, Sylvester Miller, William C. Osborn, and George Mills.

William Macy, writing on board the *Potomac* in 1841, was obviously well-educated. Over thirty years later, in retirement and nearly blind, Macy wrote and published a novel.[2] His early journal is full of literary promise, as we have already seen in 'My Island Maid,' (chapter III). His 'Description of the Scrubbing Deck' is a mock epic laden with classical allusions.

Description of the Scrubbing Deck
[H]umbug

Tis not of Eneus of Troy I sing
Nor Alexander great Macedon's King
Nor Hector's valor, nor of a Pharaoh's dream
But scrubbing decks shall be my humble theme
This first of all my subjects I will choose
To pay my simple tribute to the Muse

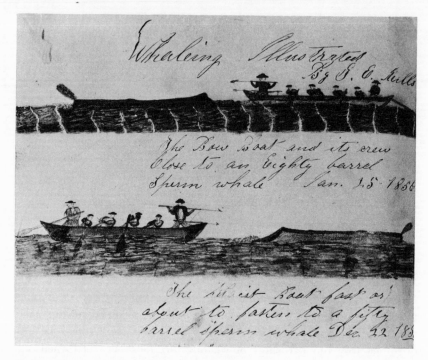

George Mills, a man of many talents, included these self-conscious pencil and watercolor sketches in his journal. They illustrate incidents Mills witnessed while a mate on board the *Java*, 1855–1856.

And simple it shall be I'll not desire
To climb Parnassus' hill, nor to her heights aspire

When first Aurora gilds the morning sky
"Draw water couple of ye" is the cry
The men roused out for scrubbing to prepare
With eyes half open snuff the morning air
Now some the ponderous drawbucket do swing
And some the sand & water forth do bring
While some the bulky scrubbroom off they drag
And others follow with boatbucket & rag
And now drawn up & ranged in fine array
Foreseeing all their labor for the day
In rank & file with a scrubbroom in their hand
Swab in silence for the dread command

And now on Boobyhatch exalted high
Stands our chief mate with stern unbending eye
With lips half open motionless as stone
"Big with the fate of Cato & of Rome"

The dreaded moment comes: the signal's given
The music of the brooms ascends to heaven
More sweet by far to aspiring whalemen's ears
Than lute or harp or music of the Spheres
And now the sluers with their buckets full
Hold the water drawers a steady pull
Dashing & throwing. swinging hit or miss
To use Salt water all their object is

And now again the mate with liberal hand
Showers away his cataracts of sand
And oftentimes while scrubbing on the deck
Some luckless wight receives it in his neck
And now a pot of ley is brought along
The men start back with horror at the sight
And wonder that the decks do grow so white
And now again the sand in vollies flows
By no means soft to cockroach – bitter foes
And running in the scuppers clogs the hole
The cry is "clear it with a scrubbroom pole"

But were I only to enumerate
All the maneuvers of our worthy mate
His throne the Boobyhatch & all its fixtures
Of lye & sand & various other mixtures
I would swell my poem to so great a size
To read it would be tedious to the eyes
Suffice to say that sand ley & wood
Are all conducive to the general good
Each has its use as part & parcel of
The mysterious process of scrubbing off

"Wash off the quarterdeck"! he cries at last
Fleet forward scrubbrooms! Head on! not too fast
The sheathing next our mate's attention claims
And sheds immortal luster on his name
To the main hatches now he shifts his post
And takes his station stately as a ghost

On the main deck the tarry is but short
For we have but time to bestow a passing thought
But "Forward there"! he cries with thundering voice
At which the men do inwardly rejoice
And forward then they bear the magic sand
Joy in their hearts & scrubbrooms in their hands
Like some poor ploughman laboring in the sod
They bend their backs with grateful thanks to God
The mate accompanies with rapid pace
And mounted on the gally takes his place
Enthroned aloft with quite sufficient room
To watch the motions of each scrubbing broom

But this part also is despatched in haste
For its most five bells we have no time to waste
With rapid motion Aft we go amain
Our former labors visiting again
At length wash down sweep up the water clean
And "Breakfast! one & all! closes the scene[3]

While the mock epic parodies only a literary type, three other writers took on specific songs or poems. Sylvester Miller, captain of the *Bayard* in 1835, modeled his 'Storm of Canal' on a song made popular by the English songwriter and showman George Alexander Stevens in 1754. Called 'Cease Rude Boreas' or 'The Storm,'[4] Stevens's song is a first-person account of a sailor's bravery in a storm at sea. Miller's version, told by a canalman maneuvering a rough passage, mocks the canalman's panic over what, to a whaleman, was a relatively minor event. Miller's version conveys the deepwater sailor's contempt for canalmen's dangers.

Storm of Canal.

1. "Hark the Captains loudly balling
Fore and aft by fendred stand
Down the scuttles quick be hauling
In the tow line hand boys hand

2. See there Charley kicks like blazes
Blow my eyes the horse is mad
Hand by Joe, he'll break his traces
Driver let him fell the gad

3. Now the dreadful thunder roaring
Hard a port – you stupid ass
On our head the rain is pouring
Steady let the mill stone pass

We've six feet water all around us
O'er our head a dirty sky
Mudy banks on both sides bound us
Hark what means that dreadful cry

Our hopes is gone our every tongue out
Our push poled washed from off the deck
A leak down in the coal hole springs out
Our vessel soon will be a wreck

Nows no time to stand and blubber
Disipate all foolish grief
Lend a hand you lazy lubber
In the stove pipe take a reef

There thats well. she walk the water
Like a thing of life afloat
Keep her steady as you ought to
And, i'll go down and change my coat[5]

Another parody was written by William C. Osborn in 1845 in the journal of William Swain, second mate on the *Citizen*. Swain must have been interested in literature, for his journal cites Moore, Burns, Shakespeare, and Byron, as well as lesser lights: Philip Snooks, Mrs. Brooks, and this whaleman. Osborn's parody plays off John G. C. Brainard's poem 'The Captain. A Fragment,' originally published in the *Connecticut Mirror*, which Brainard edited. Several anthologies reprinted 'The Captain,' including Samuel Kettel's *Specimens of American Poetry* (1829).[6] It must have had fairly wide circulation.

Brainard's poem, something of a comedy itself, tells of a captain whose ship ran afoul of a Methodist meetinghouse not far from the port of New London. This building had indeed been washed out to sea during a New England hurricane. The captain considers the many dangers of a seaman's life, but concludes that none of them equals his chance encounter with the floating meetinghouse. Osborn's version, in blank verse, is a burlesque of shore life which centers around a New Yorker's astonishment at 'the Camels,' a pontoonlike device for floating heavily laden whaleships over the bar into Nantucket harbor.

> *Parody on the "skipper's soliliquy," The New Yorker*
> *in Nantucket; & his astonishment on seeing the Camels*
>
> "*Slowly he walked along Nantucket docks,*
> *And talked of his experience.* "*I have groped*
> *In the thick night, along the muddy streets*
> *Of Albany; and I have scraped my shins*
> *O'er pairing stewes, in New Yorks devious walks.*
> *And often in my cold and lonely walk,*
> *Have heard the club armed watchmans warning tread*
> *And made my exite.*——*Aye; and I have seen*
> *The "soups" and "rowdies" fight before my nose*
> *And when they made the stones whistle like shot*
> *Have slipped away unharmed. – And I know*
> *To gain my living with a loafers skill*
> *And bear all changes with a loafers grace;*
> *But weaver yet, upon old "East," or "North,"*
> *From Sandy Hook, away up to Oyester bay,*
> *In all my rough experience of harm,*
> *Saw I the like of these.*

> *But bread, or beam, or davit, have they none*
> *Starboard nor Larboard gunwale, stem nor stern,*
> *They swim in such unthought before [?] of shape,*
> *I am afraid to board them. – Stretch out Jonas,*
> *And make for Bunkers; There, where steam-boat wharf,*
> *Fish bridge, old brant point, light house, and Cotue,*
> *Are seen in broad perspective, we'll bring up,*
> *And to our fellows there will tell the tale.*
> *How that we saw while walking out just now*
> *A new feledged two fold wonder, called "the Camels."*[7]

George Mills, always willing to try a different literary form, produced a parody. His 'Song . . . . . to Captain S. D. Oliver' is, as he notes, from Stephen Foster's 'Old Folks at Home.' Mills's description of the whales as 'wild and ugly' is probably accurate as well as comic. He decorated the margin of this page with a whale stamp, the simplified outline of a whale used in journals to mark each whale captured, perhaps out of irony or as a lucky charm.

Song . . . . . to Captain S. D. Oliver

> *Far, Far to the Arctic Ocean*
> *Where the Bow Heads Blow.*
> *There's where my mind am turning ever*
> *There's where I want to go.*
> *All this Ocean am sad and dreary*
> *Every where we stray*
> *O Captain will you go to that Ocean*
> *Go where the Bow heads Lay*
> > *Chorus . . . . .*
> *All these whales are wild and ugly*
> *All those we see*
> *O Captain will you go to that ocean*
> *Go where the Bow heads Be.*
> *All up and down this sea we've wandred*
> *Since I've been with you*

Then Captain let us go to the the Northard
There we will see something new
All the whales that are in this ocean
All are wild we see
Then Captain will you go to the Northard
To where the Bow heads Lay
All these whales, Etc

When shall I see the hills and vallyes
Far away on the Nor west shore
O Captain let us leave this ocean
And not cruise here anymore
All this ocean am sad and dreary
Every where we stray
O Captain will you go to that Ocean
Go where the Bow Heads Lay

All these whales are wild and ugly
All those we see
O Captain will you go to that ocean
Go where the Bow Heads Be.[8]

Mills had joined the ship *Leonidas* of New Bedford at Tumbez, while she was in the middle of an indifferent sperm whaling cruise.[9] His suggestion to go north to the bowhead grounds, where oil and baleen were plentiful, was apparently disregarded.

These parodies are all basically good-natured jibes – comic, but never really critical. Several examples of more vindictive humor appear in satires of life on board ship and of the whaling industry in general.

J. Goram of Nantucket satirized the Nantucket Quakers who held a virtual monopoly on whaleships sailing from that port. Nantucket Quakers were as famous for their shrewd business sense as for their piety – perhaps more.[10] Many a poor green hand arrived on the island from far inland, drawn by the imagined excitement of a whaling cruise, only to be swindled by Quaker businessmen. Melville describes just such a scene in chapter XVI of *Moby Dick*, when Ishmael signs on the *Pequod*. And many whalemen returned from long voyages with little to show for years of labor

because of the small shares the ship owners had convinced them to accept.
Goram's poem was written as his ship was bound home; he had had plenty
of time to think the matter over.

Like William Macy's 'Description of the Scrubbing Deck,' this is the
work of an educated man. Goram's heroic couplets do, in fact, pay some
small tribute to Pope, to whom he alludes.

Composed on board Ship Columbia of Nantucket by J. Goram

> *How fa' the day that e'er I left my home,*
> *And wife, and friends, on the blue sea to roam*
> *To encounter dangers, for the sake of gold*
> *And suffer hardships that can n'er be told.*
> *All you that seek for wealth, the root of evil*
> *Eschew the sea as you'd Eschew the devil*
> *And if despite advice you yet will be a Sailor*
> Let Me beseech you never try a Whaler
>
> *It little matters from what port you sail*
> *Whether from the aristocratic town you hail*
> *N. Bedford called or e'en from Marthas Isle*
> *Where herring bones that whitening pile on pile*
> *Like "Alps on alps" are in the distance seen*
> *Beware that place they'll pick you just as clean*
> *As are those bones. Then scoff at all your pains*
> *And in there pockets put your honest gains*
> *Nantucket too, a place that Fame of tells*
> *Where friendly feeling for the Stranger dwells*
> *Dwells? aye, that's a fact, it dwells and always did*
> *Beneath the smoothfaced quakers Coffin lid*
> *Its easy to detect them. When you land*
> *Whith friendly smile they extend the ready hand*
> *And greet you thus. My friend how's thee do*
> *I'm really glad to see thee; very so*
> *Thee thought thee'd come to see us, took a trip,*
> *Perhaps to see if thee could get a ship!*

I have a fine one launched the other day
She's nearly ready. I'll give thee a good lay
A good fit out I'll see thee I have to have
You'll find alas that you've been d——dly shaved
Repentance comes to late you curse and swere
But all your words are thrown to empty air
Beware the proffered hand the friendly smile
Those broad brims cover many a heart of guile
A placid face from which benevolence does shine
Serves as a pretext for roguery refined,
The abolition cause they too brefriend,
And to the wooly pates a boundless love pretend
Embrace them fondly but its all for gain
They'd steal the copper from a blind Negro's cane
Like painted sepulchers the outside is fair
When it's exposed to the worldly stare
And like them too if you could look within
You'd find a bosom filled with vice and sin
But not so all, for we are taught in schools,
There's some exceptions even to general rules,
But let me deal whith whom be it Hebrew Greek or Fakir
Heaven keep me from a Conscientious quaker[11]

A less skilled satirist, working in prose, produced six 'Rules for promotion. In the Whaling Buisneʃs.' Promotion at sea was common: illness, hard luck, desertion, and death created many opportunities for advancement. This anonymous sailor on the *China*, however, had probably just been passed over – and he was bitter about it.

Rules for promotion.
In the Whaling Buisneʃs

1st. If your Officers are easy, and condecend to take any notice of you, be sure to take every advantage of it, for it affords you an excellent opportunity to shove yourself along, especialy if you have the gift of gab; for many a clown has succeeded in the wourld with nothing but that & a little impude[nce] to the exclusion of others, both worthy & capable

2d. Have as little to do with your equals in statio[n] as possible, for every one cannot be promoted, and if you should be, it will prevent you the disagreeable trouble of cutting their future acquaintance.

3d. The most important thing to be observed, [is] your conduct towards your superiors. Keep in their company as much as possible, & persevere whether you are wanted or not; for they will soon get used to your company, & finaly think they cannot do withou[t] you.

4th. If they are talking, put in your oar, if they laugh, you laugh, and by no means be out talked or out laughed. Whay you are deficient in common sense, make up in grinning & non-sense

5th. Direct all your conversatuin to them. If you dislike any one of them, ever so much, never sh[ow] the least of it before him, but on the contrary be m[ore] humble to him, if possible, than others. There is no[thing] like having two faces, for then you can change as circumst[ances] require, & keep friends with all sides

6th. Watch all their motions, and imitate them [as] near as possible. Keep your nose as near their———backs as you can, for if they have a dirty do[?] they know who will do it without grumbling[12]

Another anonymous writer composed a song about the *Richard Mitchell* of Edgartown. His song is a virtual compendium of the possibilities for exploitation in whaling. Like Goram, this later journal keeper on the *Ocean Rover* berates the whaling management for its misplaced ideals. In this case, the author attacks the abolitionists who worked whites harder than blacks. The song was particularly timely in 1859. In 1862, the *Ocean Rover* was destroyed by the recently built Confederate ship *Alabama*, and became a casualty to the political troubles named in these verses.[13] The writer says that he will 'sing' this 'little rhyme.' It has an easy and emphatic beat and would have had an enthusiastic reception in most whaling forecastles.

I will sing you a little rhyme as I have a little time
About the meenest ship aflote in creation
Her name it is the Mitchell from E.town did sail
Where they fitted her to go to Desolation

Our officers are natives of old Cape Cod
The place where there is nothing to eat on
But the produce of their land is Mackerel bones & sand
So they had to starve or go to Desolation

On board of some ships they have plenty to eat
But it is here they put a stop on our ration
It is work for nothing & find you own grub
And starve your self to death on Desolation

The meat on this ship once belonged to a horse
Or some of his damned near relations
They put us on allowance of a quarter of a pound
They could afford no more on Desolation

For fear the flour would not last for bread three times a day
And mince pies to feed the after guards on
They cut us short one half & saying with a laugh
It's good enough for Jack on Desolation

The captains of whalers are abolitionist
They go in for Amalgamation
A nigger or a Portuguese is treated like a man
But Americans are doges on Desolation

They. cowards & villains for they were such a race
They are a disgrace to all civilization
Are our worthy friends who call them self men
And command these prison hulks on Desolation
For nards the end of the voyage they use you mighty rough
Then comes you trials & tribilations
If you have any pay they would have you run away
And pocket all your earnings on Desolation[14]

Despite an occasionally bitter tone, few writers were this resentful. Much more work was produced in a simple, comic vein, like that of Samuel Braley's poem on the death of his pig. John A. Beebe, for example, gives a much more cheerful version of the whaleman's lot even though he is describing life on a prisonlike and profitless whaling cruise.

US LONE WAND'RING WHALING-MEN

When age has rendered some old hulk
Unfit for merchant use,
She's sold at auction, bought in bulk,
Just for a whaling cruise.

Now paint and tar renews her age,
"A 1" once more stands she,
The agents then a crew engage,
Scarce half ne'er saw the sea.

With Casks in shooks, and beef and pork,
Ground tier is chocked and stowed,
The last for sailors jaws to work
The first to hold the load.

With boats, and lines and tubs prepared,
The whaler's under weigh,
To cruise where'er a ship has dared,
A floating Botany Bay.

Around the stormy southern Cape
A fearless course we steer,
Then northward, where the storm-clouds drape
The sky throughout the year.

Our cruising ground is gained, and then
Aloft loud rings the hail,
"She blows!" – look out to wind'ard men –
A ninety barrell whale.

Down go the boats – he first who can –
On for the prize we dash, –
The hunt is up, and every man
Bends or the buckling ash.

Quick! lay me on! hurra! we are fast!
Stern all! lay off, my hearts!
The monsters life is reached at last,
With lance and barbed darts.

Again long, lucklefs months go by,
And not a whale is found.
And we for better fortune try
Some other cruising ground.

Three years have sped – towards home once more
Scarcely half full of oil:
What reck we, so we gain the shore,
And tread our native soil?

Our voyage is up, and for our "lay"
We'll take wht we can get;
But find, instead of getting pay,
We're fifty cents in debt! [15]

Hiram R. King, author of 'Hone sweet hone how I love you,' celebrated
an inevitable annoyance of any whaleman's life: the vermin that infested
forecastles. Given the crowded, unsanitary conditions, 'beed bugs' and
fleas could only be controlled by predatory cockroaches. But the cure was
nearly as horrible as the disease. In *Nimrod of the Sea* (1874), Captain
William M. Davis set down some colorful entomological memories of his
early whaling days. Among other recollections, he points out that roaches
smelled bad, and left even worse smells behind them on the plates they
invariably scavenged clean.[16]

Poor Hiram King, though, suffered from an insufficiency of roaches.

One after moon When fron a Drean
I had a hard old fighting spree
With one of the Curses to man kind
that I realy Wish had left Peking

I turned in as you may suppose
Woping in sleap forge wedes
But I soon was quite Surprised
I Could not sleap or hardly close my eyes

I had such a confouned eatching
as if the thousends Devils wer fron ne leaching

but it was devels I can Swear
for Bedbugs here a plenty are

they bit ne and I killed a few
But they cepy coning fresh & new
I roaled and lunbled kicked and swore
But still the bagaers bit the nore

It is no use to for ne to quarrel
With one of the Fortunes meanes parts
I'ill leave my berth to their Descretion
And trust to heven for the rest

Now I think I'll stop rhyning
Of Such a foolish bother
For they nowe stoped upon mee Climing
I'll turn unto sone other [17]

October 8th 1854

Another comic writer, Captain Cromwell Bunker of the *Walter Scott*, made light of the customs of his Nantucket Island home, where the whaling industry affected nearly every aspect of life.

Whalers Rights

Theres a nice little Island, Just off in the sea,
With a people contented, and happy, and free ;
For whatever is said of political broil,
They go by their customs, as smothly as oil –

You must know that they got up a ball on a night,
And the folks were all smart, all the hall was all bright ;
And tw'ill furnish a clew to the thread of my ditty,
When its told they used none but the best spermaceti –

Whatever is said of politeness, in France,
The Islanders hold to the rights of the dance ;
And they care not, no more than the man in the moon,
For the landsman who never has thrown a harpoon –

The time has arrived and the company met,
And a landsman stood up at the head of a set,
But a manager told him to quit without fail;
Unless he had killed in his day a right whale. –

The man said the custom had nothing good in it,
And he'd try to enlighten their minds in a minute;
He was told twas a very nice matter to handle –
Twas like aiding the sun by the blaze of candle –

His partner declared such procedeings unfair,
As he had some pretentions among folks elsewhere;
And she'd just let them know, if she might be so bold,
He was true and straight as if run in a mould –

Then the managers saw all their customs in danger,
And they would not surrender their rights to a stranger;
So they put from the head of the dance the landlubber,
And his partner began then to cry and to blubber –

They looked very sober, the ladies and all,
And declared he would ruin the charms off the ball;
But he said he would give up his claims for that night,
As the Islanders put it in quite a new light.

Now if ever you go to that Ilse of the sea,
I advise you to take a short lesson from me:
You may be a great orator, statesman, or sailor,
But youll not lead there dances, un leſs you are a whaler. –[18]

John Jones, a whaleship steward, filled his journal entries with comic wordplay. Quite naturally, Jones emphasizes food. Every entry begins with both the date and the principal item of the dinner menu. Jones also delights in scatalogical puns, otherwise rare in whaling journals.

Friday the 9th Bean Day and of course a windy day, you might bet high on that. The first part of the day, ther was strong winds from W.N.W., Ship stearing S.W. by S., middle part light airs from the same quarter, latter part the wind come out South blowing rather fresh, the Ship heading S.E., this has ben a wet and nasty day, consequently not much doing by the mecanics, the watches came out in their Oil cloth suits, and india rubber Boots, all looking rather blue and inquiring if wee ant most round the horn, if we could only get the wind in our stern (where in fact it always ought to be, especially bean day) we might have a smart chance to get out of this in a short time, – not abloodey thing in sight[19]

Another steward, Murphy McGuire, bent many of his artistic efforts to comic descriptions of his captain. Both 'The Captain's Lament,' and 'Lines on Captain Fisher,' written many months apart, record the worries of McGuire's apparently ill-tempered captain. On 20 November 1870, McGuire imagined a view from the quarterdeck quite different from the *Ocean Rover* journalist's in 'Desolation.'

. . . . As the period of our sojourn in these parts grows shorter, our faces begin to grow longer as the time passes away without making any farther additions to our finances. The bluest man in the ship is the Captain. His conduct is decidedly unpretty. As if any one was to blame because we don't see whales. Just at present he has gone grub crazy. We eat too much. He affirms with an oath, that he never experienced such a chronic condition of eat as there is on board the "Sunbeam." In short he makes himself perfectly ridiculous. We consider a squib or two, at such persons now and then, perfectly admiſsable. Here is our latest which we have christened,

The Captain's Lament

I've sailed the seas these many years,
And knocked about a few.
But I never yet in all my life,
Had such a useleſs crew.
They know leſs, they care less,
Than any I ever saw.
They sleep more, they eat more,
Than is allowed by law.

We've been from port but fifty days,
And they've nearly bred a famine.
The way they eat the vittles up,
Is truly most alarming.

With hands full, and mouths full,
They keep their jaws in motion.
To sleep lefs, or eat lefs,
They seem to have no notion.

They've ate a ton or more of hog,
With pounds of junk Eight hundred.
And potatoes, yams, and Eufalais,
They've Eighty barrels numbered.
But they rave yet, and crave yet,
For something more to scoff.
And sleep still, and eat still,
And would if their heads were off.

Such a gang of greedy rascals,
I'm sure I never met.
And may I ever be preserved,
From such another set.
They teaze me, they craze me,
They're really very bad.
With sleeping, and with eating,
They nearly drive me mad.[20]

Later, on 14 August 1871, McGuire turned contemplative, and considered the source of Captain Fisher's foul humor.

In a reverie over the matter my muse perpetrated the following
Lines on Captain Fisher

The Captain is ugly and glum,
His face has grown skinny and pale,
Oh! what is the matter with Tom?
That he carries such lugubrious sail?

Is he thinking of friends and of home?
Of wife and of family dear?
Lamenting his having to roam,
That makes him so yellow and sere?

US LONE WAND'RING WHALING-MEN

Does he worry about his estates?
Or fret over government lands?
Or have they raised the tax rates?
That has turned him so fearfully wrong?

Is it because we are not in good luck?
And because present chances look slim?
Or do we eat too much muck?
That makes him so terribly thin.

He walks about decks in a huff,
He drones an unmeaningleſs hymn.
He cannot relish his duff,
And for variety raises rim.

He is off from his regular hash,
He won't eat good chicken stew,
To please a party so rash,
One is at a loſs to know what he can do.

In short there is nothing will please,
Do all things as well as you may,
Very best, is but poor, in his eyes,
When he's in such a miserable way.

What the cause of the trouble can be,
I really should like to know.
For a gale is half weathered, you see,
If you know which way the wind blows.

What's the use of being so sour?
Where's the need of such foolish pets!
Wry faces wont gain our desire,
Or make us the happiest yet.

Then Captain, give over your sulks,
Eat hearty, laugh loud and grow fat,
Dont fret about the results,
The feather is yet for your cap.[21]

[145]

Since creative efforts are rare in late-nineteenth-century journals, McGuire's skillful, witty verses are especially remarkable. Although there were many short comic or satiric poems about whaling life, more journalists described the trade in simple, straightforward narrative.

One of Captain Orrin Smalley's autobiographical poems reveals more than a little regret at his choice of careers. His references to God and gospel in the final stanzas are not just perfunctory. Smalley was a religious man who often recorded his misgivings about Sunday whaling. Although he claims he has told but half the story, Smalley's sorry tale should indeed 'dant the bold.'

1

When young an ocean life I began
The glittering prospects did me please
The acts and doings of many a man
Were cheering prospects of the seas

2

The style and dreſs of every seamen
The ease and pleasure of every one
In-stilled my mind with pleasing omens
And caused me to leave my happy home

3

But soon I found 'twas not so easy
The seamen themselves had me discieved
The Ocean grave is ever greedy
One half of this I'd never concieved

4

The thoughts of arriving to command
Did cheer me on my arduous life
When in that office I could command
A compensation for every Strife

5

In this as before I was descieved
I found all to be an idle dream

US LONE WAND'RING WHALING-MEN

And now for the first began to believe
That glittering dreams were seldom seen

6

Displeased with the sea and all its charms
To renounce every claim I'm ready
The pleasing prospects by me unharmed
I leave to others more bold and steady

7

My seafareing life I have given
Allow me then the whole truth to state
From whence my fears are deriven
And why the Ocean I so much hate

8

If this you will which I pray you may
Do listen then to the lines which be
And wonder not though I plainly say
An Ocean's life is no life for me

9

The sea the sea tis not for me
Its raging storms i'm loth to see
The heaving blast in swift carear
Creates in me a sadning fear

10

Its mountain seas with terror comes
Which baffles science in every form
The noble Ship so staunch and gay
To this monster becomes a prey

11

The majestic clouds so often there
In grandeur great sends sad dispair
In stealth it comes with lightning speed
In mighty form commits the deed

12
And now the scenes of hardships comes
To those who dare the Ocean rome
Their Ship a wreck and the distreſsed
Sympathy calls from every breast

13
The sea the sea tis not for me
Its rageing storms I dread to see
For in them lies a force unseen
Treacherous ever and yet sereme

14
Thus my story to you I've told
Now let others more dearing bold
The seas contend with happy glee
The Ocean great from which I'm free

15
Though bold and firm each one may be
Who now contend the rageing sea
Yet storms there are to which they'll say
All natures land has no such sway

16
When rageing mad the billows come
Declaring death in every form
Their hearts will fail they'll be dismayed
Repent the day they thus engaged

17
And thus will go imagined hopes
Which often prove a sadning hoxe
The honor gained in Ocean strife
Is paltry pay for such a life

18
Who can admire a life at sea
But such as those who foolish be

Who know no God no dangers dread
But live as though they only stayed

19
Give me the land with friends around
Churches large the Gospel sound
In-sted of seas whose honors are
delusive hopes and fleeting stars

20
And now my last to you I'll give
Concerning seas on which I've lived
Although one half has not been told
Yet sufficient to dant the bold [22]

Smalley may have been a skipper of worrisome temperament, for he had lately completed a successful voyage and was on his way to another.[23] But his worries about 'delusive hopes and fleeting stars' ultimately proved well-founded. His last three voyages from 1852 to 1864 were increasingly unlucky.[24]

Another religious captain was Clothier Peirce, given to keeping journals which consisted only of self-recriminations and prayers to the Almighty to help him catch a whale. Peirce's relentless depression, which he documented in two ongoing journals while commanding the bark *Minnesota* of New York, from 1868 to 1871, earned him notoriety. 'Crazy' Peirce, as he was nicknamed, was perhaps the fishery's ultimate pessimist.[25]

Peirce's prayers may seem a bit self-centered, especially those that make guarded promises of gifts to charity if he should get a whale. Still they achieve an almost incantatory fervor in repetition.

Lorenzo Peirce is certainly an Unfortunate Man in Whaling his Ships do not get Oil: [26] *Oh. Could this Poor Unfortunate Minnesota get One Whale this season how thankfull. I. should be I would gladly give it all for Charatable & Holy purposes. I earnestly Pray that we may yet favoured: Grant in Mercy Heavenly Parent that though unworthy that Heavens divine Blessings may Once more attend us———*

Heavenly Parent grant in Mercy that Heavens blessings may once more attend me. I pray. If I am or can be blessed to get One Whale this season: I will try to become a better Man & strive to be a Cristian for the future

July 16,

Heavenly Father grant in Mercy. I, Pray that Heavenly favours & blessings May attend this Poor and Unfortunate vessel with favour

July 18

Oh Lord in Mercy. I pray that this Poor Bark may be favoured to get One Whale is my earnest Prayer! Heavenly Father if we are but favoured I will try to be A humble and devoted Cristian

July 19, 1868

Lorenzo Peirce is certainly a ruined Man! my damnation is certain this voyage I have previously been favoured but now ruined: The Hand of devine Providence is against this Unfortunate vessel it is impossible to get One Whale We have seen Whales twice and got Nothing. I do not expect to get a Whale it seems utterly impossible for us to get One

July 26

I know that I have reached the greatest highth of my prosperity and means: I am now in the decline of Life my limited means in regard to Money is now leaving me: I shall yet be without Money or Friends in consequence of this Unfortunate voyage: I shall yet be reduced to want and beggary I know the very Hand of Providence is against us on this Voyage in consequence of my Sins and ingratitude to my Parents and Brother the Lord will Not suffer me to prosper any more – His Mercy is clean gorn for ever: all blessings are with-heald from this Poor Unfortunate vessel

Aug 1st[27]

Captain Peirce's melancholia did not prevent the *Minnesota* from stowing away a fair cargo of oil.[28] But the voyage was troubled by shipboard tension, accidents, and outright violence, perhaps brought on by the skipper's condition.[29]

Captains like Peirce who succumbed to depression were the exception. Most whalemen's writing about day-to-day life is cheerful and even optimistic. Here, for example, are six short poems from an anonymous journal keeper on the *Elizabeth* in 1837. All are concerned with the business of catching whales and make light of problems that might have sent Peirce into despair. All appear as part of the daily entries.

There was a time, (so says my rhyme,
And so 'tis prosed by many)
Sperm whales were found on " Japan Ground,"
But now there are not any.[30]

Oh, whales! Sperm Whales!
  Come, pray come!
And assist a gallant crew
Who are watching here for you
To a thousand barrels more.
Then, gales! Sweet gales!
  Come, pray, come! –
Ev'ry cloth shall woo the breeze,
While it bears us o'er the seas,
To our dearest native shore,
  To our home, "Sweet home"![31]

August! thou has not kindly been
To us lone wand'ring whaling-men:
Thou'st ta'en away from us the whales,
And left us, in their stead, strong gales,
  Rough seas, and squalls, and rain.
Let me invoke thy end may savour
Of winds and weather more in favour, –
That thy departing days may bring
(The oil to which our hopes did cling)
  Two hundred barrels gain![32]

Thankful we are for what we do receive,
But when we've nought, we're very prone to grieve: –
Give us, this season, but Five Hundred *more*,
Our thanks shall swell above old Ocean's roar.[33]

Here let me fervently our thanks express :
Indeed we're thankful for this day's success.
Hope dawns again, and bids us cease to sorrow.
O, may we take a couple more tomorrow! 34

Sperm Oil! Sperm Oil! – By patient toil our eighteenth
                                         hundred's o'er –
Reader, conceive how much we greive to want seven hundred more.
Sweep us, sweet gales, among sperm whales, till all our
                                         casks o'erflow –
Then swell the breeze, and far o'er seas our gallant bark
                                         shall go.
Haste, Time! Oh, haste! and let us taste a kindly welcome home
By those we love – and to them prove no more the main we'll
                                         roam. 35

The *Elizabeth* made home port shortly after the last of these poems was written, with a good catch: 2,200 barrels of sperm oil.36

About twenty years after the *Elizabeth* journal, Henry Cook did much the same kind of near-daily versifying at the bottom of many of his journal's pages. Together, the poems give a detailed chronicle of Cook's voyage on the *South America.*

While on the ocean i do roam
Far away from my native home
And whales we strive to find
I think of those i left behind 37

Like Jovel seamen bold
Go to our duty when told
And while lying on our pillows
The good ship bounds oer the billows 38

This is a day of meditation
According to the custom of our nation.
Papers and books we can peruse
Relating to a saviors love 39

US LONE WAND'RING WHALING-MEN

The natives look upon our ship and crew with admiration
Being but little acquainted with our nation
The Captain used the spade sharp and handle long
So as the natives should not the ship throng [40]

Now on furraign land we gaze
As about the ship we laze
Chart and compaſs we examine
That we are not on the shore stranding [41]

Those people appear to take pride
In britches low and hatbrims wide
To see the ship and crew they do admire
But to see an american woman is their harts desire
With their teeth white and their hair long
And their cerimony without a song [42]

The stated age of man
Is counted thre score years and ten
And if more time he chance to borrow
It is counted as toil and sorrow [43]

The dead both in the sea and in the ground
Must come fourth when the last trump shall sound [44]

Now we spend our leisure hours as we take a notion
As we sail upon the rageing ocean
Whether it be for or against our permotion [45]

The Ship sails through water and air
And seamen have the sails to trim and repair
And see how the land rocks and sholes bear [46]

There is danger and hardship on the seas
And sometimes we live at our ease
Being wafted along with a pleasant breeze [47]

Now we are steering towards the north pole
And many a man shivers with the cold
But we mufle up to keep us warm
And stand the brunt of cold and storm [48]

The weather with rain ice and snow
The polar whalemen have to undergo
But we look forward for the day
To cast our anchor in buzzards bay [49]

When this tedious voyage shall be oar
And we safe upon our native shore [50]

Friends and foes there we may meet
And those we love may fondly greet [51]

Now we are cruiceing in the Ochotsk sea
Not nowing our succefs may be
But our courage does not fail
That we may find and catch some whale [52]

And now we do the icey regions expore
From the unkown dep to the snow covered shore
And it does make us smile
To have a chance to get some oil [53]

Now we are in the Ochotsk sea
A killing whale to make oil are we
And if fortune does on us smile
We will be at home after a while [54]

Now we are all busey at work
Well besmeared with oil smoke and dirt
And keep a good lookout to see a whale blow
And lower away the boats and after it go [55]

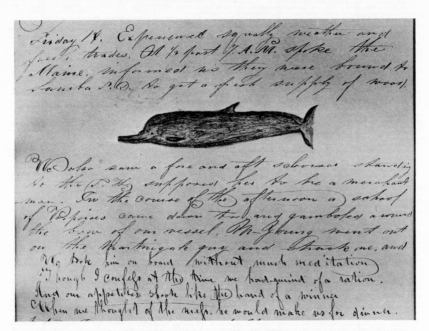

Joseph Hersey's illustrated poem about a fresh meal of sea-hog.

Now again we fall in with the fleet
And many an acquaintance here meet
To talk of the adventures upon the seas
And the transactions at home in bygon days[56]

Here the Captain and offycers try their skill
The whales to strike and their blood to spill
To take them along side and cut them in
In warm weather or cold hail snow or rain[57]

Sometimes we find it verry nice
In catching whales amongst the ice
For when we get a stoven boat
We flee to the ice that is afloat[58]

For a short time we have taken considerable oil
With much hardships fatigue and toil
But now again we have some leisure time
Wherein we can read or write or make a rime[59]

Joseph Hersey, a talented illustrator, describes a different sort of catch –
this one a bottle-nosed dolphin. Its picture accompanies Hersey's entry.

We took him on board without much meditation
Though I confeſs at the time we had mind of a ration.
And our appetites shook like the hand of a winner
When we thought of the meſs he would make us for dinner.[60]

Whalemen were generally unenthusiastic about seafood, often preferring nearly rotten salt beef to fresh fish. But many were partial to porpoise meat.

In one of his many works, Ambrose Bates, author of 'The Grandfathers Story,' greets the coming of spring to Cumberland Sound. The poem is dated April 1866, when Bates had spent more than six months on board the ice-locked *Daniel Webster*.[61] Vessels whaling the Hudson Bay area customarily spent summer on the grounds, then froze into a sheltered harbor for the winter to be on hand for floe whaling as soon as the ice broke in the spring.[62] Relatively snug in the aft section, with little to do in the long Arctic twilight, Bates probably awaited spring with impatience; April is still two months away from springtime in Cumberland Sound.

Cumberland Inlet Apr 10th 1866

When April showers. O'er naked bowers
Whir winter has defaced
Pours out their balm. So mild and calm
Along the dreary waste
Then spring time meets. Those rural sweets
Which bloom along the land
Repaying there. Our dulest care
From natures bounteous hand

Then with delight We hail the sight
Of the first flower of spring
And rais our voice. And there rejoice
At winters fleeting wing
The orb of day. Has scarce one ray
Through these dark regions cast
As flinty steel. All must congeal
And breaths the icey blast

My good Ship lay Within a bay
Of Cumberlands frozen shore
There to abide Til time and tide
Should hail old winter o'er
For day is night. Though dim twilight
May strive to light between
The frigid air. and icey glare
Soon settles o'er the scene

And now at last Old winters past
The sun comes peeping down
From distant sky. O'er mountains high
And a welcome it has found
Then let us cast Unto the blast
Three cheers by the way
And then deny Our latest cry
In winters dull decay [63]

Some writers did more than just accept their meager lot; they bragged of their accomplishments. The anonymous journalist of the ill-fated *Ocean Rover* recorded a jubilant ballad to be sung by the entire crew.

Many and trim are the whalers that appear
Acruiseing the New Holland ground over
But of all that is there there is none to compete
With the neat little Bark Ocean Rover

Cho Oh merrily merrily goes our Bark
Before the gale she bounds
So flyes the Dolphin from the shark
Or the Deer before the hounds.

2 Her movements are graceful as those of a doe
She's as fleet as a dove when in motion
And she now is acknowledged by all on the ground
To be the Pride of the Indian Ocean

cho

3 We have tryed them all under close reefed main topsail
And under top gallant sails to
But ha ha they all cry the whalers are many
But those that can beat us are few

cho

4 Now there's the Pamelia they blow on her sailing
They say she can never be beat
But whenever the Ocean Rover is round
It's then she is done up so neat

cho

5 It's not long since she was running to catch us
With her main top gallant sail out
With her mizen staysail Fly jib & Gaftopsail
But after all we had to vere about

cho

6 We first took in the main then the topsail hauled aback
and the then [sic] jib we hauled down
She couldnt catch us so the foresail we hauled up
So I'll be bugered if the Rover isnt sound

cho

7 There may be some can beat us but they must not sail slow
If they can beat us why then they blow
Was she named the Rover for she is always round
Where ever there is whalers to be found.

8 Now to finish my rhyme which is very long
She will soon be homeward bound
And if you should gam her just bear it in mind
That the rover is always round [64]

An earlier writer, W. B. Howes, devised this admiring acrostic on the name of his ship:

N oble Craft how i adore her
I n her i've rode a many a storm
M any is the time we wacht her motion
R aging billows around her foam
O nly trim her to the Wether
D ont abuse her She al proove True[65]

Stephen Easton's 'Whaling Song' gives a boastful account of the
Nantucket ship *Planter's* voyage. Many stanzas may have been adapted
from other songs. In fact, Easton probably copied his song as he listened
to a singer, since the lines are recorded carelessly, often obscuring a quite
regular ballad form. Easton's song ends with an unusual twist, warning
seamen to beware of whaling in general and one Nantucket supply house
in particular. The outfitters, Bates and Cook, must have been among the
many who sold green hands overpriced gear.

Whaling Song

1

Come all you jolly Seamen
That plough the raging main
I will tell you about Whaling where I my gold did glean
About cruising on N Zealand & in the Ochotsk Sea
The times & troubles we have had as plainly you can see

2

We sailed from Edgartown harbour[66] *the 21st of May*
Kind Neptune did protect us with a sweet & pleasant gale
Until we came around East Cape.
A storm there did arise So loudly roared the thunders
And dismal was the skies

3

We carried away our larboard boat
Likewise our davits too. our capt being a man of sense
He hove our good Ship too. we were tofsed upon the ocean
Where the wind & waters rave.
And many a jolly sailor lad did fear a watery grave

4

Our mate is a bold seaman. Jim Fisher is his name
Where danger seemed to be the most to be in it was his aim
He cheered all hands both fore and aft with a credit to his name
His name deserves to be enrolled upon the list of fame

5

But now this gale has cleared away & we have made all sail
With a fair wind for New Zealand to cruise for the spm Whale
But sperm whales are not plenty for we only took but three
And then we hauled upon the wind bound to the Ochotsk Sea

6

But now we are in the Ochotsk & in good whaling ground
It was early one fine morning we lowered all 4 boats down
Our waist boat fastened to a whale as fast as any could
And the very first lance the mate put in, he set him spouting blood

7

We soon turned up this bow-head & towed him alongside
To cut him & try him out, it was our only pride
We cut him in & tryed him out & cheerfully stowed him down
And merry were the songs we sang as we hove the windlaſs round

8

But now our ship she's full & we are bound unto our native shore
To see our wives & sweethearts, those girls we do adore –
Heres succeſs unto the Lexington. her officers & crew
And to every jolly sailor lad that wears the jacket blue *

9

Theres Bates & Cook of Nant_____ I wish I never did see
They have robbed many a sailor lad, the same as they robbed me
Its when you get on board the ship its then you'll seal your doom
They will palm you off with 3 thick shirts a heavy pot pan & spoon

10

So my boys beware of whaling beware of it in time
For if you do get overboard they will not cut the line
They will send you to Eternity if you give them a cross look
So my boys beware of Whaling likewise of Bates & Cook[67]

The end of the song is illustrated with a whale stamp for a hundred-barrel whale.

Even more detailed descriptions of a voyage are given by Reuben Ashley of the *China* in 1843. Ashley copied his song from another whaleman – perhaps in this case his brother.

the China
A song composed by James Ashley one of the Crew

1st
The China she is well rigg'd
[erasure] from New Bedford is a going
To where their is many a gale of wind my boys
And whale fish they are blowing

Chorus
So be cheerful my lads
Let your hearts never fail
Whilst the bold and saucy China
Is a cruizing after whale

2nd
It is when we do get out my boys
Oh its S.S.E. we'll steer
Till we make the Island of St Pauls
And whale fish they appear

3rd
We cruized about this country
For 2 long months or more
Till we got a thousand barrels boys
When the season it was oer

4th
We set all sail before the breeze
For the Isle of France[68] we steer'd
And left again without delay
When a sperm whale he appeared

5th

Our larboard boat all in a trice
Fasten'd without delay
they kill'd out and out my boys
And boiled her out next day

6th

It was five and thirty barrels boys
this whale it did stow down
When we set our sails so gallantly
For the Crosets we were bound

7th

We reached this cold and dreary place
On the 28th of January
And kill'd two whales but lost them both
For they sank in their flurry

8th

We cruized about this dismal spot
For two long months or more
We only took two whales my boys
And the season it was oer.

9th

We left this cold and stormy place
In the first Quarter of the moon
And reached Ottago's cruizing ground
Before the first of June

10th

We cruized about this ground my boys
For 3 long months or more
When we got 5 hundred barrels boys
And we could not get any more

11th

But we cruized around the northern ground
And fill'd her up my boy
When for new Bedford we were bound
To our hearts content and joy[69]

US LONE WAND'RING WHALING-MEN

Perhaps the best and most fully descriptive poem about whaling, and certainly the best song, is Benjamin F. Rogers's crew list poem for the schooner *V. H. Hill* in 1863. The author, an ordinary seaman, came from 'Chicargo' to join the crew he describes in his poem. Sailors of diverse backgrounds and nationalities were common on whaleships in the 1860's. This is another song that must have been sung by the entire crew. Tactfully – perhaps wisely – Rogers omits descriptions of the officers.

Poem by B F Rogers

it was the 14th day of April
i remember well the day
as our gallang little schoonr
lay at anchor in the bay
our hearts were light and bouyant
as we striped ourselfs for toil
it is heave up the anchor boys
and of we go for oil

there is manuel and two Johns
Making three in all
They are the Valient Portuegues
From the island of Fayal
There wants must be attended to
By Gleason or else Bill
For they are the gay Boatsteerers
of the schooner Varnum Hill

In speaking of the Portuguse
I thought i'de said enough
I will mention the young steward
For he gives us Pork and duff
And soft tack he gives us to
As much as ere we please
Oh spare a place in Heaven
For the blackeyed Portugues

AND THE WHALE IS OURS

There are twelve of us before the mast
Three have been to sea before
There is Ebe and Sam and seaman Jack
From the yankee man of war
And Tom and Jim and Gleason
Charley George Steve Frank and Bill
For we are the gallus Bummers
Of the schoonr Varnum Hill

First before the mast comes Jack
From some Southern state
Before we sailed from Provincetown
He said he would be mate
But to talk about such things
It seames all very nice
He shipped as able seaman
And can neither reef or splice

Next comes Sam a Boston Chap
Who is some among the girls
His hair is Black as midnight
And hangs in graceful curles
Once before he's been a whaleing
And cruised round center bay
He made 12 & 30 cents
And got the 150 lay

Ebe hails from New Hamshire
And been to the Black Sea
He also went to China
Where we get our Hongkong tea
But when we go to Faial
And anchor safe and sound
we will go ashore together
And take a drink around

The largest man before the mast
George Kelley he by name

US LONE WAND'RING WHALING-MEN

He fought in Buells army
And came back home quite lame
But now he thinks that Whaleing
Is more needful than the sword
And he will fight no longer
In the army of the Lord

There is Bill he is quite a genius
And from the west he came
He did not like the country
And is he much to blame
He thought he'd be a sailor
And plough the raging main
But if he once gets home again
He will never come again

Tom is a miskcheavous chap
He came from Ballyrooe
He sailed in a packet ship
From Cork to Liverpool
He came to America
Sweet Freedom to enjoy
He is the sprig of a shelaiegh
And the broth of a boy

Next in rhyme comes Jimmy
He is one of the boys
He plays with Stephens Windmill
And vairous other toys
He worked in a glass house
But did not learn to Blow
He came from that happy land
Called Canida & Oh

How are you gay young Gleason
All the way from York
Oh what a mug has he boys
For stowing Beef and Pork

And when it is his watch on deck
Against the windlass he will set
And as often as he falls asleep
As often he gets wet

How are you next little Frank
Some sixteen years of age
He is the smalest boy aboard
His surname it is Page
He draws water for the steward
For he has to clean no craft
He gets the cakes and puddings
The steward brings from aft

There is Steve the Nova Scotian
He can eat his weight in sails
He blows about Victoria
Likewise the Prince of Wales
He grumbles continually
From morning untill he is asleep
He is the shape of a dolpin
And has scales upon his feet

The last in line comes Charley
But though last he is not least
He has three hairs upon his head
And come from way down east
He thought he'd be a soldier
And go down to Bull Run
And when he returned again
Twas with two fingers and a thumb

I must not forget the Cook
If he is so very slow
He gives us soft tack every day
And that is mostly dough
He has a high and lively gait
About as fast i think

As a Mississippi Crockodile
Going down to drink

Now comes your humble servant
B Frank Rogers you all know
His fighting weight is 7 stone 10
And he came from Chicargo
And when the Voyage is over
to the westward we will steer
And never go so far again
From Whisky and Lager Beer

And when we all return again
To drift on the sea of Life
Or each has settled down
And taken to himself a wife
And when the final day arrives
We will bow to Heavens high will
Memory will bring back the hours
Spent on the schooner Varnum Hill[70]

George Gould, a carpenter on the *Columbia* in 1841, was the only whaleman journalist to try his hand at playwriting. His untitled drama of a whale hunt appears in the back of his journal, complete with stage directions. Such complete description is rare in journals, although common in published books and letters to hometown newspapers. Gould had a good ear for the language of his shipmates, and recorded their dialects and trade talk faithfully. The drama achieves a sense of immediacy, perhaps because it was a kind of transcript of an actual catch. Gould's sole concern is for the business of the chase. There is little character development, and no intrigue. The strength of Gould's drama lies in his accurate presentation of an exciting reality.

Commenced these twenty four hours with a fine brease heading S.S. East for the Marquesas Islands. the watch on deck had Struck four bells. the man at the wheal and mast heads had been relieved but a few moments before the man up forwards Sang out   there She Breaches

[167]

Capt –	*Where away*
	Four points off the larbard bow Sir
Capt	*How far off*
	Six miles Sir
Capt	*Keep her off three points there, Square in the Main yards And Mizen topsail*
Crew	*Aye Aye Sir*
Capt	*Then belay all that. haul the topsail brace a Small pull then belay all, Haul the Weather fore topsail brace a Small pull, jump up there a Couple of you And rig out the fore top mast Studing Sail Boom. Bear a hand men if you love Money.*
Crew	*Aye Aye Sir. (And a Couple jumped into the Weather fore rigen. When the mate from the Main topmast head Sang out there She blows Close aboard Sir*
Capt	*What do they look like*
Mate	*Sperm Whales Sir! there She blows. there She ripples regular old Logs*
Capt	*How are they headed*
Mate	*Square to leeward Sir. Slow as night*
Capt	*Bring the Ship to the Wind there. Brace up the fore and mizen topsails. Haul aback the Main yard. Call all hands*

The Main yard was backed. And the hoarse And unwelcome Sounds of all hands ahoy brought us on deck

Capt	*Do you See Anything of the Whales there*
Mate	*No Sir. they have gone down*
Man forward.	*There She Blows. one point forward of the lee Beam sir*
Capt –	*Come down there from aloft. Clear away the boats*
2d Mate	*Here Cook Stand by My Boat*
Cook	*Aye Aye Sir*
Mates	*Stand by the boats here.*
Capt	*Hoist and Swing the Cranes all ready there*
Mates	*Aye Aye Sir*
Capt	*Lower away then*
2d Mate	*Come be lively follow her down men bully boat you know, waste boat forever, bend in your line there. down to your oars*

This watercolor from George Gould's *Columbia* journal complements his
short dramatization of whaling life.

men, line your oars. Now give her a good Stroke. forwards
with her. will you beat that boat. you can do it. only Say So.
And the Whale is ours. What say now a fresh start I will give
you all I have but my wife, do men lay back.

Boat Steerer	*They have gone down Sir*
2d Mate	*Heave up. there peak your oars. take your paddles men*
Boat Steerer	*Signal from the Ship Sir. Whales are up there She blows Sir*
	one point on Starbord bow
2d Mate	*I see them, take your oars men, What say men give her a good*
	Start? only one mile off. Will you pull. a bottle of rum for
	every man, What say. there they lay still as night. Waiting
	for us. there we come up with them hand over hand
Boat Steerer	*Whale on lee beam Sir*
2d Mate	*Take out your oars. look out for the Sail Warren*
B. Steerer	*Aye Aye Sir let it Come*
2d Mate	*Loose the Sail, pass off the Sheat take your paddles men that*
	Whale is ours
B. Steerer	*As you go Sir, Steady,*
2 Mate	*Lay down you paddles men and Stand by your oars easy men.*
	Stand up Warren

the Whale was but a few feet from us   Warren Stood up With the iron in his
hand waiting for orders

2d Mate	Paddle men one foot More And he is ours. What are you looking over your Sholeders for I will look out for the Whale. do paddle one foot more. ready there Warren?
B Steerer	Aye Aye Sir
2d Mate	Give it to him then

And the Boat Steerer burried two irons to the Sockets

| 2d Mate | Stern all, Stern all. I tell you. ever mother Son of you. Stern. Wett line there. trim boat. look out that you do not Crab your oars. hold on hard every one of you. hold on. there She fights. haul line Men. Come aft Warren. |
| B Steerer | Aye Aye Sir |

the Boatsteerer goes aft And the 2d Mate goes forward

| 2d Mate | Now haul line men. with a will Stand by your oars men. Bowman Stand by to haul the line. haul I tell you haul. pull I tell you there he fights Sixty bbl fellow haul I tell you one good chance and I will Settle his hash for him. (darts his lance) Stern all. Stern all I tell you, Stern if you wish to See Nantucket |

the Whale had now gone down and the boat lay in Bloody water. all looking out and waiting for the Whale to rise, he come up the boat happend to be in his way And he Stove her abaft the bow thwart

| 2d Mate | Stern you lubbers Stern, Stern I tell you. Stern all to the Devil, off Shirt one of you tear up the Scaling one of you And stuff in your Shirts there. there that's the talk. Now we are off again Haul line bullies Now's your time there he lays like a log. oh do haul will you men. I will pay for your Shirts. (darts his lance) |

The Whale then rounded too And come for the boat the 2d Mate Sung out Stern but it was to late he stove us again and We Could Not Stuff it up with Shirts, the 2 Mate And two of the Crew jumped overboard. the Whale ran to leeward a Short distance went into his flurry, headed to the Sun[71] and turned fin out,

An aftermath of a whaling encounter, as executed by journalist Joseph Hersey. With his hat still in place, the unruffled officer seems to have seized the opportunity to deliver a lecture on what went wrong.

2d Mate	*Jump in Men in to the boat, the danger is all gone. rig out your oars athart ship and we will weather her out. Curse old leper I thought the bloody buger Would leave me in Davy Jones locker. Set the wafes head and Stern. the old Man will Soon pick us up. Keep her headed to windward there Warren. the bloody think Can t Sink Men. Rather wet here boys. but you will feell better after you get dry. we'll Splice the main brace to pay for this*
Crew	*Sail ho! dead a head heading as we Stern. the old Man comeing to pick us up Boys*

after backing and filling for a long time he ran down to us

Capt	*Take in your oars. how do you expect to get along Side*
2d Mate	*If I take them in She will capsize I think Sir*
Capt	*I don't Care take them in I tell you Who Shiped you to think?*

The old rule is. Obey orders if you break boners. in Comes the oars And over goes the boat. Every one for himself And the Devil for us all.

Capt.	*There you have done it now. oh! you Sap heads. well jump in. Come up here Stands by to take up the waste boat. all ready to hoist there*
2d Mate	*Aye Aye Sir, all ready*
Capt	*Hoist away there fore and aft. lively men up with her, there high, put her on the Cranes, coil up the falls.*

Mate	Clew up the Mizen topsail here
Crew	Aye Aye Sir
Mate	Belay the weather clewling Start away the lee Sheet. Belay lee clewling. jump there and furl him
Crew	Aye Aye Sir
Mate	Clew down the fore Topsail, there
Crew	Aye Aye Sir
Mate	Let go the haliards. round down on your Clewlings. haul your reeftacles. there belay all. let him hang for the present Haul down the jibs.
Crew	Aye Aye Sir
Mate	Man the Downhauls let go the Halliards Belay all. jump there and furl them, this way all of you. off Fore hatches jump down and pass up the Cutting gear. jump up in the Main Top and heave down the Cutting pennants one of you. overhaul you tacle for the Cutting falls
Man	Aye Aye Sir
Mate	Stand by here to hoist. hoist away there
Crew	Aye Aye Sir (Shanty boys)
	Was you ever in Kennebec hey Storm along
	Brouseing timber round your deck Storm along Stormy
Mate	That's the talk lively men. high. overhaul your fall And up with the other. bear a hand Men
Capt	Bear a hand then, on Monkey rope And over in the Whale overhaul your Cutting falls.
Boat Steerer on the Whale	Overhaul on deck bear a hand
Capt	There now is your time. hook in
Boat Steerer	Kill them bloody Sharks Sir. they will take off my leg yet
Capt	Kick them in the eye, Kick them in the eye. hoist, hoist, I tell. heave and Lunge. heave men, round, round. Slip Slap, that's the talk, five and forty more
Crew	Round round men Main yard him Com you darky open your Smelling bottle heave one, heave all. heave you bloody Kanaka heave. Steward give us Some Nantucket grog. (Water with

Molasses And Sawdust in it) Splice the main brace every mothers Son.

Capt   *Heave Men last Blanket piece tore of his jacket. And yet aknother. that the last jump up and send down the falls. off Main hatches and down with the blubber. off the Cobboose Cover Men and on Case.*

Mate   *Rig the minceing horse and fill the tubs there here Cook give us some fire here. Strike a light under the pots and give her old hallet*

B Steerer   *Aye Aye Sir*

Mate   *here Cooper, how are you off for casks?*

Cooper   *All right Sir, pleanty of them*

B Steerer   *Clean Strainer here one of you*

Crew   *you go Jim I cleaned it last. blow me if I do though. you are hard aboard of it. (Mad) Damn the bloody old Ship hope She will Sink. Never mind home Soon.*

2d Mate   *What are you growling about thare. like a dog with a Sore head. bare a hand or I will light you along with a ropes end you bloody old Mahone Soldier.*

B Steerer   *More Scraps here one of you that the kind. pleanty of them. Most twelve To Man at the Wheel Eight Bells. Call the watch*[72]

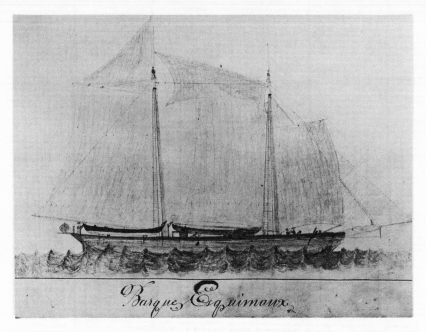

In addition to verse, Joseph Hersey's 1843 journal includes this wash drawing of his vessel, the schooner *Esquimaux*.

What the whalemen wrote about daily life and whaling is the most interesting of all the creative writing in the logs and journals. But there is one astounding omission. In all the daily entries, great and small, describing whaling encounters, the object of the hunt was almost ignored. Details of whale behavior or appearance not related directly to the catch did not interest whalemen, who found their inspiration in other occupational topics. Whaling journalists occasionally referred to such legendary rogue sperm whales as the notorious Mocha Dick or Timor Tom, but Melville's mystique about whales, which may postdate his whaling career, was extraordinary in more ways than one. Speculations like Ahab's about the essence or personality of a whale are almost nonexistent in whaling manuscripts. Elizabeth Morey's quaint reflections (chapter IV), like the lady herself, are a remarkable, though minor, exception.

In describing their occupational lives, whalemen were relatively free from standard format and diction. Gone were the emotional restraints that fostered generalizations or platitudes about such potentially painful subjects as home, love, and death. Describing the specific details of life at sea could be done without anguish. In general, the writers avoid the perils of inbred trade jargon as well. A better humor and a keener eye, unblinded by clichés, yield a closer look at elements of life on board a whaleship.

AFTERWORD

THESE journals show what a nonprofessional writer in Victorian times could produce, especially when writing about scenes and action which he knew first-hand. Of course, whaling had been described in fictionalized narratives and newspaper accounts of the whalechase itself and visits to colorful foreign ports, but the pictures painted were exotic and thrilling. These descriptions ignored the sordid aspects of whaling life and its frequent monotony, for neither would have made good copy for back-home consumption.

Ironically, the heroes of this escape literature designed for those on shore were themselves leading dull lives at sea, only occasionally relieved by patches of grueling work, excitement, danger, and visits to the seamier sections of foreign ports. Their daily life led them to seek escapes of their own, both in reading and in writing. Initially, at least, much of their writing was triggered by boredom, not the traditional literary ideal of inspiration.

On the whole, the writing of these whalemen journalists resembles that of their contemporaries. All were encouraged by the same trends and influenced by the same reading. All followed traditional literary forms to express the emotions their society thought proper. Indeed, much of the shipboard writing that deals with the themes of home, love, and death can scarcely be separated from that which was being written on shore.

The whalemen avoided only two of the major themes of their day, temperance and patriotism, both of which are political as well as literary concerns. Perhaps the whalemen lacked interest in these issues, which so involved landsmen, because of their distance from shore and the propaganda there. But that is only part of the answer; newspapers and such were sometimes available, though often out of date. Their avoidance of the subject of temperance is completely understandable, for alcohol was one of the whalemen's only too few pleasures. Condemning that would have meant condemning themselves to an even more monotonous life. The whalemen's detachment from the fervid nationalism that was almost a way of life for many of their fellow Americans is more striking. Although many journalists describe July 4th shipboard celebrations, community life at sea was clearly more important than political life at home. Perhaps some of the whalemen's best work was the result of rechanneling energies ordinarily devoted to patriotism.

Much Victoriana is marked by excessive emotion: pathos, melodrama, farce. Whalemen were not free from these extremes, as George Mills's 'The Orphan Child,' Ambrose Bates's tale of Tookalooky, and William Wilson's 'Queen of Otaheite' abundantly illustrate. It is in writing about whaling that whalemen differ most in style from their contemporaries on shore. When they turned their attention to the activities of their daily life, they became more spontaneous, more personal, more original. Here, the whalemen's geniality, cheerfulness, and good humor generally prevail – rare virtues for the age.

Comedy is generally considered a young man's mode, and the men on Yankee whaleships were certainly young. But more significantly, comedy is concerned more with man's place within his group or society than with him as an individual, and the life of whalemen, both in the cabin and the forecastle, was necessarily class-structured and communal. What is surprising is that the exploitive nature of the industry and the long, forced association of men in cramped quarters evoked so little open bitterness. Only a few writers, most notably the *Ocean Rover* journalist who produced 'Desolation,' and J. Goram, the author of the most detailed anti-Nantucket gibes, crossed the line from comedy into satire.

Some of their work, of course, is inadvertently comic, simply because the writers lack control. They are unaware of the effects produced by juxtaposing the light and the ordinary with the grave and the solemn. John Cleland's memorable line, 'some bubbles arose from his place of repose' is a classic example.

Another of the whalemen's qualities, again atypically Victorian, is their relative simplicity, which often may be attributed to lack of education rather than aesthetic choice. Again, it is in the writing about whaling that the virtue is most obvious. Here, comparatively speaking, the journalists avoid the superabundance of elevated and pompous diction which has helped to stigmatize the word 'Victorian.'

AFTERWORD

Most of the examples in this anthology, besides seeing print for the first time, have probably been read by fewer than ten people since their authors set them down in their private journals; their novelty adds to the pleasure of reading them. But their ultimate worth is much greater than the charm which their freshness, good humor, and simplicity all contribute to. The work of these creative writers gives a whole new perspective on a special vocation – nineteenth-century American whaling – that until now has been discussed in almost entirely impersonal terms. Historians, economists, and sociologists have been concerned primarily with dates, profits, and other statistics of the industry. For the most part, literary critics have limited themselves to *Moby Dick*, especially its allegory. The poetry, the drama, and the fiction these journalists produced give a glimpse into the individual lives of the men who actually went whaling.

Their writing is at its best where it is most illuminating for the modern reader: not in the scenes of home, love, and death, where they have little to add to what their contemporaries wrote, but in the one area in which they could speak as real experts. When whalemen wrote about whaling, they did not romanticize it. Their fresh, exuberant writing celebrated their unusual life in pursuit of the whale.

NOTES

PREFACE

1. Benjamin F. Rogers, Journal Kept on Board Schooner *V. H. Hill* of Provincetown, 1863 (The Kendall Whaling Museum, Sharon, Mass. [hereafter KWM]).
2. Stuart C. Sherman, *The Voice of the Whaleman with an Account of the Nicholson Whaling Collection* (Providence, R.I.: Providence Public Library, 1965), p. 32.
3. Richard M. Hixson, Journal Kept on Board Ship *Maria* of Nantucket, 1832–1834 (by permission of the Houghton Library, Harvard University, Cambridge, Mass.). Hixson was a member of the Sharon, Mass., Lyceum (*Sharon, Massachusetts: A History* [Sharon, Mass.: Sharon American Revolution Bicentennial Committee, 1976]).

CHAPTER ONE

1. Elmo P. Hohman, *The American Whaleman: A Study of Life and Labor in the Whaling Industry* (New York, London, and Toronto: Longmans, Green and Co., 1928), pp. 48–49. Hohman gives 1830 as the turning point in the growth of whaling from small-town undertakings to full-scale industry.
2. *Ibid.*, pp. 289–301.
3. Sherman, p. 25.
4. Private conversation with Stuart C. Sherman, Sharon, Mass., 13 September 1977.
5. Private conversation with William Kranzler, New Bedford, Mass., August 1974.
6. George Edgar Mills, Journal Kept on Board Bark *Java* of New Bedford, 1855; Ship *Leonidas* of New Bedford, 1856; and Bark *Mary Francis* of Warren, 1856 (KWM), 15 February 1856.
7. Hohman, pp. 57–58.
8. Kenneth R. Martin, *Delaware Goes Whaling 1833–1845* (Greenville, Del.: The Hagley Museum, 1974), p. 17.

9. Hohman, p. 48.
10. John A. States, Journal Kept on Board Ship *Nantasket* of New London, 1845–1846 (Manuscript Collection, Mystic Seaport, Inc., Mystic, Conn. [hereafter MS]).
11. *Whalemen's Shipping List and Merchants' Transcript* (New Bedford), 9 April 1867 (hereafter *Whalemen's Shipping List*).
12. Ambrose H. Bates, Journal Kept on Board Bark *Milwood* of New Bedford, 1867–1868; and Brig *Isabella* of New Bedford, 1868 (KWM).
13. R. G. N. Swift, Journal Kept on Board Ship *Contest* of New Bedford, 1866–1868, 1868–1870 (KWM).
14. *Whalemen's Shipping List*, 22 May 1866 and 22 December 1868.
15. Swift Journal (KWM), entry before 15 December 1868.
16. Hohman, p. 215.
17. For a collection of such songs, see Gale Huntington, *Songs the Whalemen Sang* (Barre, Mass.: Barre Publishers, 1964), chapter one. However, Huntington regularizes much of the verse and includes a number of examples from merchantmen.
18. Edouard Stackpole, *The Sea Hunters: The New England Whalemen During Two Centuries, 1635–1835* (Philadelphia: J. B. Lippincott Company, 1953), p. 270.
19. Eliza S. Brock is an interesting example, though many of the poems she records are copied. See her Journal Kept on Board Ship *Lexington* of Nantucket, 1853–1856 (Peter Foulger Museum, Nantucket Historical Association, Nantucket, Mass. [hereafter PFM/NHA]).
20. Elizabeth H. Morey, Journal Kept on Board Ship *Phoenix* of Nantucket, 1853–1856 (PFM/NHA).
21. Fanny Fern was the pseudonym of Sarah Payson (Willis) Parton, a best-selling writer of short sentimental and comic sketches. See her collection, *Fern Leaves from Fanny's Port-folio* (Auburn: Derby and Miller: Buffalo: Derby, Orton and Mulligan; [etc., etc.], 1853).
22. Meade Minnigerode, *The Fabulous Forties, 1840–1850* (Garden City, N.Y.: Garden City Publishing Co., Inc., 1924), pp. 107, 115.
23. The works of lesser writers, other than such well-known poets as Mrs. Felicia Hemans, Mrs. Lydia Sigourney, and the Misses Alice and Phoebe Carey, are difficult to find today. The enthusiast can enjoy Michael Turner's *Parlour Poetry: A Casquet of Gems* (New York: The Viking Press, 1969).
24. James D. Hart, *The Popular Book; A History of America's Literary Taste* (New York: Oxford University Press, 1950), p. 155.

NOTES

25. For an extended discussion of reading on whaleships, see Pamela A. Miller, "What the Whalers Read," *Pages*, I (1976): 242–247.
26. Francis Allyn Olmsted, *Incidents of a Whaling Voyage, to which are added Observations on the Scenery, Manners and Customs, and Missionary Stations of the Sandwich and Society Islands,* etc. (New York: D. Appleton and Co., 1841), p. 52.
27. J. Ross Browne, *Etchings of a Whaling Cruise, with Notes of a Sojourn on the Island of Zanzibar, to which is appended a Brief History of the Whale Fishery,* etc. (New York: Harper & Brothers, Publishers, 1846), pp. 110–111.
28. Frederick H. Russell, Journal Kept on Board Bark *Pioneer* of New Bedford, 1873; 1875–1876 (Sterling Library, Yale University, New Haven, Conn.).

CHAPTER TWO

1. William H. Stimpson, Journal Kept on Board Ship *Minerva* of New Bedford, 1844–1847 (Nicholson Whaling Collection, Providence Public Library, Providence, R.I. [hereafter NWC/PPL]).
2. Mills Journal (KWM), 29 May 1856.
3. Samuel G. Swain, *in* Stephen Easton, Jr., Journal Kept on Board Ship *Planter* of Nantucket, 1852–1855 (Collection of the International Marine Archives, Nantucket, Massachusetts [hereafter IMA]), 29 November 1849.
4. J. Goram, *in* George Gould, Journal Kept on Board Ship *Columbia* of Nantucket, 1841–1844 (KWM).
5. *Ibid.*, 4 December 1845.
6. Hiram R. King, Journal Kept on Board Bark *Fortune* of New Bedford, 1854–1856 (KWM), 1 October 1854.
7. Samuel T. Braley, Journal Kept on Board Ship *Arab* of Fairhaven, 1849–1852 (KWM), 3 February 1850.
8. *Ibid.*, 31 December 1849.
9. Ambrose H. Bates, Journal Kept on Board Bark *Milwood* of New Bedford, 1867–1868 (KWM).
10. *Ibid.*
11. Franklin Tobey, Journal Kept on Board Ship *Atlantic* of Nantucket, 1846–1849 (PFM/NHA).
12. Ambrose H. Bates, Journal Kept on Board Schooner *U.D.* of Fairhaven, 1868–1869 (NWC/PPL).
13. Mills Journal (KWM).

CHAPTER THREE

1. William A. Weeden, Journal Kept on Board Ship *John & Edward* of New Bedford, 1841–1844 (IMA).
2. Frederick H. Smith, Journal Kept on Board Bark *Petrel* of New Bedford, 1871–1874 (KWM), 22 February 1873, but after 22 August 1873 entry.
3. *Ibid.*, 22 March 1874, but after 22 August 1873 entry.
4. Bates *U.D.* Journal, 1868–1869 (NWC/PPL).
5. William Silver, Journal Kept on Board Ship *Bengal* of Salem, 1832–1835 (Essex Institute, Salem, Mass.).
6. Joseph E. Ray, Journal Kept on Board Ship *Edward Cary* of Nantucket, 1854–1858 (PFM/NHA), dated 3 December 1857, but after 7 June 1856 entry.
7. William H. Macy, Journal Kept on Board Ship *Potomac* of Nantucket, 1841–1845 (MS).
8. William H. Wilson, Journal Kept on Board Bark *Cavalier* of Stonington, 1848–1850 (MS).
9. Hohman contends that abusive profanity was so prevalent in the trade that forecastle hands became altogether indifferent to it. Yet profanity is markedly absent from the journals. As with pornography, it is probable that the conventions of the times combined with shore censorship to eliminate profanity from journals. Hohman pp. 123–124.
10. Index of New Bedford Whalemen and Seamen. Melville Whaling Room, New Bedford Free Public Library, New Bedford, Mass.
11. George Howland, Journal Kept on Board Bark *Pioneer* of New Bedford, 1875–1877 (KWM), 22 April 1877. It is interesting to note that 'Leubin' is an eighteenth-century name associated with a rural clown type, and the work may have antique sources.
12. Samuel T. Braley, Journal Kept on Board Ship *Arab* of Fairhaven, 1845–1849 (KWM), 14 July 1848.
13. *Ibid.*, no date.
14. *Ibid.*
15. *Ibid.*
16. Samuel T. Braley, Journal Kept on Board Ship *Arab* of Fairhaven, 1850–1852 (KWM).
17. *Ibid.*, 4 February 1850.
18. Samuel T. Braley, Journal Kept on Board Ship *Arab* of Fairhaven, 1852–1853 (KWM), 13 January 1853.
19. Federal Writers Project of the Works Progress Administration of the State

NOTES

of Massachusetts, *Whaling Masters*, American Guide Series (New Bedford, Mass.: Old Dartmouth Historical Society, 1938); Alexander Starbuck, *History of the American Whale Fishery from Its Earliest Inception to the Year 1876* (1878; reprint ed., 2 vols., New York: Argosy-Antiquarian Ltd., 1964).

20. Mills Journal (KWM).
21. *Ibid.*, 4 March 1856.
22. Bates refers here to the *Hecla* and the *Fury*, Royal Naval vessels under the celebrated Captain Edward Parry, which searched for a northwest passage in 1824–1825. (David Mountfield, *A History of Polar Exploration* [New York: The Dial Press, 1974], pp. 76–78.) Bates necessarily sets the scene at a date well before his own time, but the *Hecla* and *Fury* detail helps establish credibility in a setting that might otherwise seem fantastic.
23. Here, Bates's use of the first person and his personal connections enhance his story's credibility. But this time, he is fabricating. The *Milwood* cruised the Indian and Pacific Oceans in the period he refers to; and in any case Bates was not aboard her ('Bark Milwood of New Bedford,' in Dennis Wood, Abstracts of Whaling Voyages from the United States, 1831–1873, 7 vols., New Bedford Free Public Library, New Bedford, Mass. [hereafter NBFPL], III, 208).
24. Bates, *Milwood/Isabella* Journal (KWM).

CHAPTER FOUR

1. Frederick Law Olmsted, cited earlier, had been pursuing a medical career. Plagued by ill health, he shipped on a whaler as a passenger to seek a more therapeutic climate. (Olmsted, p. iv.)
2. Henry W. Balch, M. D., *The Seamen's Medical Guide, A Treatise on Various Diseases, with Directions for Treatment . . . When a Physician Cannot be Procured* (New York: Epes Sargent, 1850), pp. 58–59, 89–90, 83–84.
3. Henry M. Bonney, Journal Kept on Board Ship *William Badger* of Lynn, 1845–1849 (MS), 19 February 1847.
4. Mills Journal (KWM), 10 May 1856.
5. Kenneth R. Martin, 'Wilmington's First Whaling Voyage, 1834–1837,' *Delaware History*, XVI, 2 (1974): 153–170.
6. *Ibid.*, 165.
7. John Cleland, Jr., Journal Kept on Board Ship *Ceres* of Wilmington, 1834–

1837 (The Mariner's Museum, Newport News, Va.), 30 August 1836; quoted in Martin, 'Wilmington's First Whaling Voyage, 1834–1837,' 165.

8. Lorenzo Dow Baker, Journal Kept on Board Ship *Romulus* of Mystic, 1851–1854 (MS), 15 October 1853.

9. *Ibid.*, 17 November 1854.

10. J. Goram, in Gould Journal (KWM), 15 November 1845.

11. Orrin Smalley, Journal Kept on Board Ship *Minerva* 2nd of New Bedford, 1848–1850 (Melville Whaling Room, NBFPL), 26 November 1850.

12. *Ibid.*, 23 November 1850.

13. *Ibid.*

14. Angles Snell, Journal Kept on Board Bark *Bevis* of New Bedford, 1850–1853 (KWM), 20 November 1850.

15. *Ibid.*, Journal Kept on Board Bark *Alto* of New Bedford, 1854–1857 (KWM).

16. *Ibid.*, *Bevis* Journal (KWM), 28 November 1850.

17. Mills Journal (KWM), 27 May 1856.

18. Edwin C. Pulver, Journal Kept on Board Ship *Brutus* of Warren, 1854–1856; 1857–1859 (NWC/PPL).

19. Braley, *Arab* Journal, 1849–1852 (KWM), 8 June 1850.

20. Morey Journal (PFM/NHA), 2 October 1854.

21. *Ibid.*, 8 March 1854.

CHAPTER FIVE

1. Constance Rourke, *American Humor, A Study of the National Character* (1931: reprint ed., Garden City, N.Y.: Doubleday Anchor Books, Doubleday & Company, Inc., 1953), p. 101.

2. In 1877, Macy published a barely fictionalized account of a whaling voyage: *There She Blows! or, The Log of the Arethusa* (Boston: Lee & Shephard, Publishers; New York: Charles T. Dillingham, 1877). It is a minor whaling classic.

3. Macy Journal (MS).

4. Huntington, p. 72.

5. Sylvester Miller, Journal Kept on Board Ship *Bayard* of Greenport, 1835–1837 (MS).

6. Samuel Kettel, *Specimens of American Poetry, with Critical and Biographical Notices*, vol. III (Boston: S. G. Goodrich & Co., 1829), 205.

7. William C. Osborn, *in* William H. Swain, Journal Kept on Board Ship *Citizen* of Nantucket, 1844–1846 (IMA), 1 January 1845.

8. Mills Journal (KWM).

NOTES

9. Alexander Starbuck, *History of the American Whale Fishery from Its Earliest Inception to the Year 1876* (1878: reprint ed., 2 vols., New York: Argosy-Antiquarian Ltd., 1964), 514–515.
10. Hohman, p. 10.
11. Goram, *in* Gould Journal (KWM).
12. Journal Kept on Board Ship *China* of New Bedford, 1840 (The Peabody Museum of Salem, Salem, Mass.).
13. Starbuck, 570–571.
14. Journal Kept on Board Ship *Ocean Rover* of Mattapoisett, 1859 (Old Dartmouth Historical Society and Whaling Museum, New Bedford, Mass. [hereafter ODHSWM]).
15. John A. Beebe, Journal Kept on Board Bark *Governor Carver* of New Bedford, 1854–1857; and Bark *Tropic Bird* of New Bedford, 1857–1859 (PFM/NHA).
16. William M. Davis, *Nimrod of the Sea; or, The American Whaleman* (New York: Harper & Brothers, Publishers, 1874), pp. 326–327.
17. King Journal (KWM), 8 October 1854. Ironically, the captain of the *Fortune* on this voyage was Henry W. Beetle, and the owner or agent James Beetle (Starbuck, 514). Perhaps the wordplay was intentional.
18. Cromwell Bunker, Journal Kept on Board Ship *Walter Scott* of Nantucket, 1840–1844 (PFM/NHA), 6 November 1842. A popular novel of the period celebrates the same custom. See Joseph C. Hart, *Miriam Coffin; or, The Whale-Fisherman, A Tale* (2nd ed., 2 vols., New York: Harper & Brothers. 1835).
19. John Jones, Journal Kept on Board Ship *Eliza Adams* of New Bedford, 1852; Ship *Roman* of New Bedford, 1853–1854; and Ship *Sea* of New Bedford, 1854–1855 (KWM).
20. Murphy McGuire, Journal Kept on Board Bark *Sunbeam* of New Bedford, 1868–1871 (ODHSWM), 20 November 1870.
21. *Ibid.*, 14 August 1871.
22. Smalley, *Minerva* 2nd Journal (NBFPL), 20 November 1850.
23. Starbuck, 422–423, 454–455.
24. *Ibid.*, 492–493, 534–535, 574–575.
25. Charles Boardman Hawes found one of Peirce's journals almost unrivaled in the annals of melancholy; see his *Whaling* (Garden City, N.Y.: Doubleday, Page & Co., 1924), p. 240. This view was supported by A. Hyatt Verrill in *The Real Story of the Whaler: Whaling Past and Present* (New York and London: D. Appleton and Company, pp. 169–71), and 'James Stick in the Mud, Esq., From New Bedford, Mass. [pseud.]' in his essay,

'Of Whalemen's Laments,' *The Bulletin Old Dartmouth Historical Society and Whaling Museum*, Spring 1957, p. 1.

26. Lorenzo, Clothier's brother, was the *Minnesota's* agent (Hawes, p. 239; Starbuck, 631).

27. Clothier Peirce, Jr., Journal Kept on Board Bark *Marion* of New Bedford, 1862–1863; and Bark *Minnesota* of New York, 1868–1871 [?]; *in* John Jones, Journal Kept on Board Ship *Eliza Adams* of New Bedford, 1852; Ship *Roman* of New Bedford, 1853; and Ship *Sea* of New Bedford, 1854–1855 (KWM).

28. One might suppose from these woebegone entries that God had turned a deaf ear to Captain Peirce. In fact, He answered the skipper's prayers more than once. By March 1869, the *Minnesota* had taken three sperm whales, one giant of which yielded 120 barrels of oil ('Bark Minnesota of New York,' in Dennis Wood, Abstracts of Whaling Voyages from the United States, 1831–1873 [7 vols., NBFPL], IV, 359.) Providential assistance did not, however, moderate Captain Peirce's litany.

29. Hawes, pp. 248–250; Starbuck, 630–631.

30. Journal Kept on Board Ship *Elizabeth* of Dartmouth, 1837–1841 (KWM), 30 August 1838. The Japan Grounds were the whaling waters of the western North Pacific.

31. *Ibid.*, 16 June 1839.

32. *Ibid.*, 22 August 1839.

33. *Ibid.*, 4 September 1839. The figure cited refers to barrels of oil.

34. *Ibid.*, 20 September 1839.

35. *Ibid.*, 11 February 1840.

36. Starbuck, 336–337.

37. Henry Cook [?], Journal Kept on Board Bark *South America* of New Bedford, 1853; 1856–1857 (KWM), 5 January 1853.

38. *Ibid.*, 10 January 1853.

39. *Ibid.*, 16 January 1853 (a Sunday).

40. *Ibid.*, 21 January 1853. *South America* lay uneasily at one of the Ryukyu Islands, only four months ahead of Commodore Perry's historic arrival to protect American seamen.

41. *Ibid.*, 23 January 1853.

42. *Ibid.*, 1 February 1853.

43. *Ibid.*, 8 February 1853.

44. *Ibid.*, 14 February 1853.

45. *Ibid.*, 23 February 1853.

46. *Ibid.*, 6 March 1853.

47. *Ibid.*, 15 March 1853.

48. *Ibid.*, 24 March 1853.

49. *Ibid.*, 30 March 1853.

50. *Ibid.*, 8 April 1853.

51. *Ibid.*, 17 April 1853. Items 51, 52, 53, although appearing in entries for different days, are probably meant to be read as a single poem.

52. *Ibid.*, 24 April 1853.

53. *Ibid.*, 1 May 1853.

54. *Ibid.*, 13 May 1853.

55. *Ibid.*, 19 May 1853.

56. *Ibid.*, 26 May 1853.

57. *Ibid.*, 31 May 1853.

58. *Ibid.*, 3 June 1853.

59. *Ibid.*, 11 June 1853.

60. Joseph B. Hersey, Journal Kept on Board Schooner *Esquimaux* of Province-town, 1845–1846 (KWM), 14 April 1843 [sic].

61. *Whalemen's Shipping List*, 23 May 1865; 'Ship Daniel Webster of New Bedford,' in Dennis Wood, Abstracts of Whaling Voyages from the United States, 1831–1873 [7 vols., NBFPL], IV, 42.

62. W. Gillies Ross, *Whaling and Eskimos: Hudson Bay 1860–1915*, National Museum of Man Publications in Ethnology, No. 10 (Ottawa: National Museums of Canada, National Museum of Man, 1975), pp. 51–53.

63. Bates, *U.D.* Journal (NWC/PPL), 10 April 1866.

64. *Ocean Rover* Journal (ODHSWM).

65. W. B. Howes, Journal Kept on Board Ship *Nimrod* of Sag Harbor, 1841–1842 (MS).

66. Nantucket whaleships often cleared from Edgartown.

67. Stephen Easton, Jr., Journal Kept on Board Ship *Planter* of Nantucket, 1852–1855 (IMA), March 1853. This song was probably recorded after a gam with the *Lexington*.

68. Mauritius.

69. James Ashley, *in* Reuben Ashley, Journal Kept on Board Ship *China* of New Bedford, 1843–1845 (NBFPL).

70. Rogers Journal (KWM). A crew list in the journal gives the complete names of the twenty-one members of the crew and officers.

71. Whales headed to the sun to die frequently enough to become a motif in whaling folklore.

72. George Gould, Journal Kept on Board Ship *Columbia* of Nantucket, 1841–1844 (KWM), 23 February 1844.

BIBLIOGRAPHY

UNPUBLISHED SOURCES

ASHLEY, JAMES *in* ASHLEY, REUBEN. Journal Kept on Board Ship *China of* New Bedford, 1843–1845. Melville Whaling Room, New Bedford Free Public Library, New Bedford, Mass.

BAKER, LORENZO DOW. Journal Kept on Board Ship *Romulus* of Mystic, 1851–1854. Manuscript Collection, Mystic Seaport, Inc., Mystic, Conn.

BATES, AMBROSE H. Journal Kept on Board Bark *Milwood* of New Bedford, 1867–1868; and Brig *Isabella* of New Bedford, 1868. The Kendall Whaling Museum, Sharon, Mass.

Journal Kept on Board Schooner *U.D.* of Fairhaven, 1868–1869. Nicholson Whaling Collection, Providence Public Library, Providence, R.I.

BEEBE, JOHN A. Journal Kept on Board Bark *Governor Carver* of New Bedford, 1854–1857; and Bark *Tropic Bird* of New Bedford, 1857–1859. Peter Foulger Museum, Nantucket Historical Association, Nantucket, Mass.

BONNEY, HENRY M. Journal Kept on Board Ship *William Badger* of Lynn, 1845–1849. Manuscript Collection, Mystic Seaport, Inc., Mystic, Conn.

BOODRY, BENJAMIN L. Journal Kept on Board Ship *Arnolda* of New Bedford, 1852–1855. Old Dartmouth Historical Society and Whaling Museum, New Bedford, Mass.

BRALEY, SAMUEL T. Journal Kept on Board Ship *Arab* of Fairhaven, 1845–1849. The Kendall Whaling Museum, Sharon, Mass.

Journal Kept on Board Ship *Arab* of Fairhaven, 1849–1852. The Kendall Whaling Museum, Sharon, Mass.

Journal Kept on Board Ship *Arab* of Fairhaven, 1852–1853. The Kendall Whaling Museum, Sharon, Mass.

BROCK, ELIZA S. Journal Kept on Board Ship *Lexington* of Nantucket, 1853–1856. Peter Foulger Museum, Nantucket Historical Association, Nantucket, Mass.

BUNKER, CROMWELL. Journal Kept on Board Ship *Walter Scott* of Nantucket, 1840–1844. Peter Foulger Museum, Nantucket Historical Association, Nantucket, Mass.

CLELAND, JOHN, JR. Journal Kept on Board Ship *Ceres* of Wilmington, 1834–1837. The Mariner's Museum, Newport News, Va.

COOK, HENRY [?]. Journal Kept on Board Bark *South America* of New Bedford, 1853, 1856–1857. The Kendall Whaling Museum, Sharon, Mass.

EASTON, STEPHEN, JR. Journal Kept on Board Ship *Planter* of Nantucket, 1852–1855. Collection of the International Marine Archives, Nantucket, Mass.

GORAM, J. *in* GOULD, GEORGE. Journal Kept on Board Ship *Columbia* of Nantucket, 1841–1844. The Kendall Whaling Museum, Sharon, Mass.

GOULD, GEORGE. Journal Kept on Board Ship *Columbia* of Nantucket, 1841–1844. The Kendall Whaling Museum, Sharon, Mass.

HARCOURT, JOHN BERTRAM. 'Themes of American Verse, 1840–1849; A Survey of the Volumes from that Period Contained in the Harris Collection of American Poetry in Brown University.' 2 vols. Ph.D. dissertation, Brown University, Providence, R.I., 1952.

HERSEY, JOSEPH B. Journal Kept on Board Schooner *Esquimaux* of Province-town, 1845–1846. The Kendall Whaling Museum, Sharon, Mass.

HIXSON, RICHARD M. Journal Kept on Board Ship *Maria* of Nantucket, 1832–1834. By permission of the Houghton Library, Harvard University, Cambridge, Mass.

HOWES, W. B. Journal Kept on Board Ship *Nimrod* of Sag Harbor, 1841–1842. Manuscript Collection, Mystic Seaport, Inc., Mystic, Conn.

HOWLAND, GEORGE. Journal Kept on Board Bark *Pioneer* of New Bedford, 1875–1877. The Kendall Whaling Museum, Sharon, Mass.

Index of New Bedford Whalemen and Seamen. Melville Whaling Room, New Bedford Free Public Library, New Bedford, Mass.

JONES, JOHN. Journal Kept on Board Ship *Eliza Adams* of New Bedford, 1852; Ship *Roman* of New Bedford, 1853–1854; and Ship *Sea* of New Bedford, 1854–1855. The Kendall Whaling Museum, Sharon, Mass.

Journal Kept on Board Ship *China* of New Bedford, 1840. The Peabody Museum of Salem, Salem, Mass.

Journal Kept on Board Ship *Elizabeth* of Dartmouth, 1837–1841. The Kendall Whaling Museum, Sharon, Mass.

Journal Kept on Board Ship *Ocean Rover* of Mattapoisett, 1859. Old Dartmouth Historical Society and Whaling Museum, New Bedford, Mass.

KING, HIRAM R. Journal Kept on Board Bark *Fortune* of New Bedford, 1854–1856. The Kendall Whaling Museum, Sharon, Mass.

MACY, WILLIAM H. Journal Kept on Board Ship *Potomac* of Nantucket, 1841–1845. Manuscript Collection, Mystic Seaport, Inc., Mystic, Conn.

MCGUIRE, MURPHY. Journal Kept on Board Bark *Sunbeam* of New Bedford, 1868–1871. Old Dartmouth Historical Society and Whaling Museum, New Bedford, Mass.

BIBLIOGRAPHY

MILLER, SYLVESTER. Journal Kept on Board Ship *Bayard* of Greenport, 1835–1837. Manuscript Collection, Mystic Seaport, Inc., Mystic, Conn.

MILLS, GEORGE EDGAR. Journal Kept on Board Bark *Java* of New Bedford, 1855; Ship *Leonidas* of New Bedford, 1856; and Bark *Mary Frances* of Warren, 1856. The Kendall Whaling Museum, Sharon, Mass.

MOREY, ELIZABETH H. Journal Kept on Board Ship *Phoenix* of Nantucket, 1853–1856. Peter Foulger Museum, Nantucket Historical Association, Nantucket, Mass.

OSBORN, JAMES C. Journal Kept on Board Ship *Charles W. Morgan* of New Bedford, 1841–1844. Manuscript Collection, Mystic Seaport, Inc., Mystic, Conn.

OSBORN, WILLIAM C. *in* SWAIN, WILLIAM H. Journal Kept on Board Ship *Citizen* of Nantucket, 1844–1846. Collection of the International Marine Archives, Nantucket, Mass.

PEIRCE, CLOTHIER. Journal Kept on Board Bark *Marion* of New Bedford, 1862–1863 and Bark *Minnesota* of New York, 1868–1871 [?]. *In* Jones, John, Journal Kept on Board Ship *Eliza Adams* of New Bedford, 1852; Ship *Roman* of New Bedford, 1853–1854; and Ship *Sea* of New Bedford, 1854–1855. The Kendall Whaling Museum, Sharon, Mass.

PROVOST, JOHN. Journal Kept on Board Ship *Alexander* of Nantucket, 1827–1831. Peter Foulger Museum, Nantucket Historical Association, Nantucket, Mass.

PULVER, EDWIN C. Journal Kept on Board Ship *Brutus* of Warren, 1854–1856, 1857–1859. Nicholson Whaling Collection, Providence Public Library, Providence, R.I.

RAY, JOSEPH E. Journal Kept on Board Ship *Edward Cary* of Nantucket, 1854–1858. Peter Foulger Museum, Nantucket Historical Association, Nantucket, Mass.

ROGERS, BENJAMIN F. Journal Kept on Board Schooner *V. H. Hill* of Provincetown, 1863. The Kendall Whaling Museum, Sharon, Mass.

RUSSELL, FREDERICK H. Journal Kept on Board Bark *Pioneer* of New Bedford, 1873; 1875–1876. Sterling Library, Yale University, New Haven, Conn.

SILVER, WILLIAM. Journal Kept on Board Ship *Bengal* of Salem, 1832–1835. Essex Institute, Salem, Mass.

SMALLEY, ORRIN. Journal Kept on Board Bark *Isabella* of New Bedford, 1852–1855; and Bark *Hecla* of New Bedford, 1856–[?]. Melville Whaling Room, New Bedford Free Public Library, New Bedford, Mass.

Journal Kept on Board Ship *Minerva* 2nd of New Bedford, 1848–1850. Melville Whaling Room, New Bedford Free Public Library, New Bedford, Mass.

SMITH, FREDERICK H. Journal Kept on Board Ship *Herald* of New Bedford, 1865–1866. The Kendall Whaling Museum, Sharon, Mass.
Journal Kept on Board Bark *Petrel* of New Bedford, 1871–1874. The Kendall Whaling Museum, Sharon, Mass.

SMITH, VARAMUS. Journal Kept on Board Ship *Ohio* of Nantucket, 1841–1844. Manuscript Collection, Mystic Seaport, Inc., Mystic, Conn.

SNELL, ANGLES. Journal Kept on Board Bark *Alto* of New Bedford, 1854–1857, The Kendall Whaling Museum, Sharon, Mass.
Journal Kept on Board Bark *Bevis* of New Bedford, 1850–1853. The Kendall Whaling Museum, Sharon, Mass.

STATES, JOHN A. Journal Kept on Board Ship *Nantasket* of New London, 1845–1846. Manuscript Collection, Mystic Seaport, Inc., Mystic, Conn.

STEDMAN, CHARLES. Journal Kept on Board Ship *Mount Wollaston* of New Bedford, 1853–1855. Melville Whaling Room, New Bedford Free Public Library, New Bedford, Mass.

STIMPSON, WILLIAM H. Journal Kept on Board Ship *Minerva* of New Bedford, 1844–1847. Nicholson Whaling Collection, Providence Public Library. Providence, R.I.

SWAIN, SAMUEL G. *in* EASTON, STEPHEN, JR. Journal Kept on Board Ship *Planter* of Nantucket, 1852–1855. Collection of the International Marine Archives, Nantucket, Mass.

SWIFT, R. G. N. Journal Kept on Board Ship *Contest* of New Bedford, 1866–1868, 1868–1870. The Kendall Whaling Museum, Sharon, Mass.

TOBEY, FRANKLIN. Journal Kept on Board Ship *Atlantic* of Nantucket, 1846–1849. Peter Foulger Museum, Nantucket Historical Association, Nantucket, Mass.

WEEDEN, WILLIAM A. Journal Kept on Board Ship *John & Edward* of New Bedford, 1841–1844. Collection of the International Marine Archives, Nantucket, Mass.

WILSON, WILLIAM N. Journal Kept on Board Bark *Cavalier* of Stonington, 1848–1850. Manuscript Collection, Mystic Seaport, Inc., Mystic, Conn.

WOOD, DENNIS. Abstracts of Whaling Voyages From the United States, 1831–1873. 7 vols. Melville Whaling Room, New Bedford Free Public Library, New Bedford, Mass.

BIBLIOGRAPHY

PUBLISHED SOURCES

ASHLEY, CLIFFORD W. *The Yankee Whaler*. Boston: Houghton Mifflin Company, 1926.

ABRAHAMS, ROGER D., and FOSS, GEORGE. *Anglo-American Folksong Style*. Englewood Cliffs, N.J.: Prentice Hall, 1968.

BALCH, HENRY W., M.D. *The Seamen's Medical Guide, a Treatise on Various Diseases, with Directions for Treatment . . . When a Physician Cannot be Procured*. New York: Epes Sargent, 1850.

BARRY, PHILLIPS; ECKSTORM, FANNIE HARDY; and SMYTH, MARY WINSLOW. *British Ballads from Maine: The Development of Popular Songs with Texts and Airs*. New Haven, Conn.: Yale University Press, 1929.

BARRY, PHILLIPS, ed. *The Maine Woods Songster*. Cambridge, Mass.: The Powell Printing Co., 1939.

BLAIR, WALTER. *Native American Humor (1800–1900)*. New York: American Book Company, 1937.

BODE, CARL. *Antebellum Culture*. 1959. Reprint. Carbondale and Edwardsville, Ill.: Southern Illinois University Press, 1970.

BRANCH, E. DOUGLAS. *The Sentimental Years, 1836–1860*. 1934. Reprint. New York: Hill and Wang, 1965.

BRONSON, G. W. *Glimpses of the Whaleman's 'Cabin.'* Boston: Damrell & Moore, Printers, 1855.

BROWN, HERBERT ROSS. *The Sentimental Novel in America, 1789–1860*. Durham, N.C.: Duke University Press, 1940.

BROWNE, J. ROSS. *Etchings of a Whaling Cruise, with Notes of a Sojourn on the Island of Zanzibar, to which is appended a Brief History of the Whale Fishery*, etc. New York: Harper & Brothers, Publishers, 1846.

COLCORD, JOANNA C. *Songs of American Sailormen*. New York: W. W. Norton & Company, Inc., 1938.

CRAPO, HENRY H. *The New-Bedford Directory, containing the Names of Inhabitants . . . the Town Register*, etc. New Bedford, Mass.: Press of Benjamin Lindsey, 1845.

CREIGHTON, HELEN. *Maritime Folk Songs*. Toronto: Ryerson Press, 1962.

DALZIEL, MARGARET. *Popular Fiction 100 Years Ago; An Unexplored Tract of Literary History*. London: Cohen & West, 1957.

DAVIS, WILLIAM M. *Nimrod of the Sea; or, The American Whaleman*. New York: Harper & Brothers, Publishers, 1874.

DOERFLINGER, WILLIAM M. *Shanteymen and Shanteyboys: Songs of the Sailor and Lumberman*. New York: The Macmillan Co., 1951.

ECKSTORM, FANNIE HARDY, and SMYTH, MARY WINSLOW. *Minstrelsy of Maine: Folksongs and Ballads of the Woods and the Coast.* Boston and New York: Houghton Mifflin Co., 1927.

ELY, BEN-EZRA STILES. *'There She Blows': A Narrative of a Whaling Voyage in the Indian and South Atlantic Oceans.* 1849. Reprint. Edited by Curtis Dahl. Middletown, Conn.: Published for the Marine Historical Association, Incorporated, by Wesleyan University Press, 1971.

FAXSON, FREDERICK WINTHROP. *Literary Annuals and Gift Books; A Bibliography with a Descriptive Introduction.* Boston: The Boston Book Company, 1912.

Federal Writers Project of the Works Progress Administration of the State of Massachusetts. *Whaling Masters.* American Guide Series. New Bedford, Mass.: Old Dartmouth Historical Society, 1938.

FLANDERS, HELEN HARTNESS, and OLNEY, MARGUERITE. *Ballads Migrant in New England.* New York: Farrar, Straus and Young, 1953.

FIEDLER, LESLIE. *Love and Death in the American Novel.* Rev. ed. New York: Stein and Day, 1966.

GRISWOLD, RUFUS WILMOT, ed. *The Female Poets of America.* Philadelphia: Carey and Hart, 1849.

GRISWOLD, RUFUS. *The Poets and Poetry of America, With an Historical Introduction.* 2nd ed. Philadelphia: Carey and Hart, 1842.

HALEY, NELSON COLE. *Whale Hunt: The Narrative of a Voyage by Nelson Cole Haley, Harpooner, in the Ship Charles W. Morgan, 1849–1853.* New York: Ives Washburn, Inc., 1948.

HARLOW, FREDERICK PEASE. *Chanteying Aboard American Ships.* Barre, Mass.: Barre Gazette, 1962.

HART, JAMES D. *The Popular Book; A History of America's Literary Taste.* New York: Oxford University Press, 1950.

HART, JOSEPH C. *Miriam Coffin; or, The Whale-Fisherman. A Tale.* 2nd ed. 2 vols. New York: Harper & Brothers, 1835.

HAWES, CHARLES BOARDMAN. *Whaling.* Garden City, N.Y.: Doubleday, Page & Company, 1924.

HEFLIN, WILSON L. 'New Light on Herman Melville's Cruise in the *Charles and Henry*.' *Historic Nantucket*, vol. 22, no. 2 (1974): 6–27.

HOHMAN, ELMO P. *The American Whaleman: A Study of Life and Labor in the Whaling Industry.* New York, London and Toronto: Longmans, Green and Co., 1928.

HUGILL, STAN. *Shanties From The Seven Seas; Shipboard Work-Songs and Songs used as Work-Songs from the Great Days of Sail.* London: Routledge & Keegan Paul; New York: Dutton, 1961.

BIBLIOGRAPHY

HUNTINGTON, GALE. *Songs The Whalemen Sang*. Barre, Mass.: Barre Publishers, 1964.

JAMES, LOUIS, ed. *English Popular Literature, 1819–1851*. New York: Columbia University Press, 1976.

JAMES, LOUIS. *Fiction for the Working Man, 1830–1850; a Study of the Literature Produced for the Working Classes in Early Victorian Urban England*. New York: Oxford University Press, 1963.

JOHNSON, BARBARA. 'The Lure of the Whaling Journal.' *Manuscripts*, XXIII, 3 (1971): 159–177.

KETTEL, SAMUEL. *Specimens of American Poetry, With Critical and Biographical Notices*. 3 vols. Boston: S. G. Goodrich and Co., 1829.

LAWRENCE, MARY CHIPMAN. *The Captain's Best Mate; The Journal of Mary Chipman Lawrence on the Whaler Addison, 1856–1860*. Edited by Stanton Garner. Providence, R.I.: Brown University Press, 1966.

LAWS, G. MALCOLM, JR. *American Balladry from British Broadsides; A Guide for Students and Collectors of Traditional Song*. Publications of the American Folklore Society, Bibliographical Series, vol. 8. Philadelphia: American Folklore Society, 1957.

Native American Balladry; A Descriptive Study and a Bibliographical Syllabus. rev. ed. Publications of the American Folklore Society, Bibliographical and Special Series, vol. 1. Philadelphia: The American Folklore Society, 1964.

LEVY, LESTER S. *Flashes of Merriment: A Century of Humorous Songs in America 1805–1905*. Norman, Okla.: University of Oklahoma Press, 1971.

Grace Notes in American History: Popular Sheet Music from 1820–1900. Norman, Okla.: University of Oklahoma Press, 1967.

LINSCOTT, ELOISE HUBBARD. *Folk Songs of Old New England*. New York: The Macmillan Company, 1939.

MACY, CAPT. W. H. *There She Blows! or, The Log of the Arethusa*. Boston: Lee & Shephard, Publishers, 1877.

MARTIN, KENNETH R. *Delaware Goes Whaling, 1833–1845*. Greenville, Del.: The Hagley Museum, 1974.

'Wilmington's First Whaling Voyage, 1834–1837,' *Delaware History*, XVI, 2 (1974): 152–170.

MELVILLE, HERMAN. *Moby-Dick; or, The Whale*. New York: Harper & Brothers, Publishers; and London: Richard Bentley, 1851.

MILLER, PAMELA A. 'What the Whalers Read.' *Pages*, I (1976): 242–247.

MINNIGERODE, MEADE. *The Fabulous Forties, 1840–1850*. Garden City, N.Y.: Garden City Publishing Co., Inc., 1924.

MORISON, SAMUEL ELIOT. *The Maritime History of Massachusetts, 1783–1860*. Boston: Houghton Mifflin Company, 1921.

MOTT, FRANK LUTHER. *Golden Multitudes: The Story of Best Sellers in the United States*. New York: The Macmillan Company, 1947.

'MUD, JAMES STICK IN THE, ESQ., From New Bedford, Mass. [pseud.]' 'Of Whalemen's Laments.' *The Bulletin Old Dartmouth Historical Society and Whaling Museum*, Spring 1957, pp. 1–3.

MURPHY, CHARLES. *A Journal of a Whaling Voyage on Board Ship Dauphin, of Nantucket*. Mattapoisett, Mass.: Published by The Atlantic Publishing Company, 1877.

National Archives Project. *Ship Registers of New Bedford, Massachusetts*. 3 vols. Compiled by the Survey of Federal Archives, Division of Professional and Service Projects, Works Projects Administration. The National Archives, Cooperating Sponsor. Boston: The National Archives Project, 1940.

NOEL, MARY. *Villains Galore, The Heyday of the Popular Story Weekly*. New York: Macmillan, 1954.

OLMSTED, FRANCIS ALLYN. *Incidents of a Whaling Voyage, to which are added Observations on the Scenery, Manners and Customs, and Missionary Stations of the Sandwich and Society Islands*, etc. New York: D. Appleton and Co., 1841.

PATTEE, FRED LEWIS. *The Development of the American Short Story, An Historical Survey*. New York and London: Harper & Brothers, 1923.
The Feminine Fifties. New York: D. Appleton-Century Company, Incorporated, 1940.

PEARSON, EDMUND. *Dime Novels; or, Following an Old Trail in Popular Literature*. Boston: Little, Brown and Co., 1929.
Queer Books. Garden City, N.Y.: Doubleday, Doran and Company, Inc., 1928.

RICKETSON, ANNIE HOLMES. *The Journal of Annie Holmes Ricketson on the Whaleship A. R. Tucker, 1871–1874*. Foreword by Philip F. Purrington. New Bedford, Mass.: The Old Dartmouth Historical Society, 1958.

RIEGEL, ROBERT E. *Young America, 1830–1840*. Norman, Okla.: University of Oklahoma Press, 1949.

ROSS, W. GILLIES. *Whaling and Eskimos: Hudson Bay 1860–1915*. National Museum of Man Publications in Ethnology, no. 10. Ottawa, Ontario: National Museums of Canada, National Museum of Man, 1975.

ROURKE, CONSTANCE. *American Humor, A Study of the National Character*. 1931. Reprint. Garden City, N.Y.: Doubleday Anchor Books, Doubleday & Company, Inc., 1953.

SAGENDORPH, ROBB. *America and her Almanacs*. Boston: Little, Brown and Company, 1970.

The Sailors' Magazine. (The organ of the American Seamen's Friend Society.) Published monthly at New York. Volumes I–XLV, 1828–1873.

BIBLIOGRAPHY

SCAMMON, CHARLES M. *The Marine Mammals of the North-western Coast of North America: Together with an Account of the American Whale Fishery.* 1874. Reprint. New York: Dover Publications, Inc. 1968.

Sharon, Massachusetts: A History. Sharon, Mass.: Sharon American Revolution Bicentennial Committee, 1976.

SHERMAN, STUART C. *The Voice of the Whaleman with an Account of the Nicholson Whaling Collection.* Providence, R.I.: Providence Public Library, 1965.

SKALLERUP, HARRY R. *Books Afloat & Ashore.* Hamden, Conn.: Archon Books, 1974.

SPEARS, JOHN R. *The Story of the New England Whalers.* New York: Macmillan Company, 1908.

SPAETH, SIGMUND. *A History of Popular Music in America.* New York: Random House, 1948.

STACKPOLE, EDOUARD. *The Sea Hunters: The New England Whalemen During Two Centuries, 1635–1835.* Philadelphia: J. B. Lippincott Company, 1953.

STARBUCK, ALEXANDER. *History of the American Whale Fishery from Its Earliest Inception to the Year 1876.* 1878. Reprint. 2 vols. New York: Argosy-Antiquarian, Ltd., 1964.

TOMPKINS, J. M. S. *The Popular Novel in England 1770–1800.* London: Constable & Company, 1932.

TRIPP, HOWLAND. *In Whaling Days.* Boston: Little, Brown and Company, 1909.

TURNER, MICHAEL R., ed. *The Parlour Song Book: A Casquet of Vocal Gems.* New York: The Viking Press, 1973.

Parlour Poetry: A Casquet of Gems. New York: The Viking Press, 1969.

VERILL, A. HYATT. *The Real Story of the Whaler: Whaling, Past and Present.* New York and London: D. Appleton and Company, 1929.

VINCENT, HOWARD P. *The Trying-out of Moby-Dick.* Boston: Houghton Mifflin Company, 1949.

Whalemen's Shipping List and Merchants' Transcript. Published weekly at New Bedford, Mass., from 17 March 1843 to 29 December 1914.

WHITING, EMMA MAYHEW; and HOUGH, HENRY BEETLE. *Whaling Wives.* Boston and Cambridge, Mass.: Houghton Mifflin Company, The Riverside Press, 1953.

WILLIAMS, HAROLD, ed. *One Whaling Family.* Boston and Cambridge, Mass.: Houghton Mifflin Company, The Riverside Press, 1964.

WINSLOW, OLA ELIZABETH. *American Broadside Verse from Imprints of the 17th & 18th Centuries.* New Haven, Conn.: Yale University Press, 1930.

INDEX

INDEX

AND THE WHALE IS OURS

This book has been set in Monotype Ehrhardt
by William Clowes & Sons of England. Ehrhardt
is a stout and sturdy Dutch face named after the
famed Leipzig foundry in which it was first cut
in 1686. It maintains the same characteristics that
Joseph Moxon found so attractive in the 'late
made Dutch letters' which he found appealing
for 'the commodious Fatness they have beyond
other Letters, . . . As also the true placing their
Fats and their Leans, with the sweet driving
them into one another.' In other words, he found
both their shape and their fit admirable.

Designed by Howard I. Gralla, printed and
bound at The Murray Printing Company of
Forge Village, Massachusetts, on Monadnock
Text, laid finish paper.